The
Houdini
Conspiracy

The Crusade against Spiritualism

Christopher G. Owen

Archway Publishing books may be ordered through booksellers or by contacting:

Archway Publishing
1663 Liberty Drive
Bloomington, IN 47403
www.archwaypublishing.com
844-669-3957

ISBN: 978-1-6657-1249-1 (sc)
ISBN: 978-1-6657-1250-7 (hc)
ISBN: 978-1-6657-1281-1 (e)

Library of Congress Control Number: 2021919764

Print information available on the last page.

Archway Publishing rev. date: 09/30/2021

To Sue and Maisy.

Contents

Authors Note

And they lived happily ever after … Such is not the ending to the stories of the pioneer spiritualists. All of this is due to the hidebound skeptics. The king of those was the so-called handcuff king, Erik Weisz, a.k.a. Harry Houdini. He was a Hungarian-born immigrant. In 1924 he published a book entitled *A Magician among the Spirits*. It was a venomous, totally biased, and cynical work, a diatribe using every possible piece of defamatory gossip or information capable of one being able to look at through a negative lens. And all the time Houdini kept up a false front that he was impartial, just a fair-minded seeker of the truth for the general public. All the while, however, he was a confirmed hypocrite who offered thousands of dollars for a demonstration of genuine mediumship where he, of course, would be judge and jury, the sole arbiter of what constituted such a thing. Such a prize he should have awarded to Mina Crandon for the time he got caught red-handed trying to sabotage one of her critical séances for the *Scientific American* committee. He sat on that committee of scientists, even though he wasn't an educated scientist himself and was not qualified to be there by any stretch. His chief qualification was that he was an international showman and a blowhard who intimidated the other scientists into turning a lukewarm eye onto the phenomena that Crandon produced. Houdini's influence cheated Crandon out of the *Scientific American* magazine's prize. Even after Houdini's attempted sabotage, the committee still allowed him a vote on the prize, which was ridiculously unfair for them to do. He voted in the negative, of course.

Almost a century has passed since the real Houdini, the man whose words dripped with contempt and jealousy for a religion that was not his own and which he never considered genuine, became the greatest scourge and menace to that religion in the public eye. And looking back over that time through hindsight we can conclude that it was a mission accomplished for Houdini. He set out to take down the religion of spiritualism and it looks convincingly like he did so. Although pockets of the once great movement still exist, it is a movement that is still under attack from within and without. It is the embers of what once was a great bonfire that swept the world. Much, if not all, of this is due to the successful negative publicity extravaganza of the great international superstar Houdini. He was the darling of the press. He carried on a great personal crusade all the way to the United States Congress to outlaw one of the world's great religions.

In a tolerant society one would think that the public would look down upon such a man who was a religious bigot and scoundrel in his dealings with the spiritualists. But because of the prevailing positive press narrative of that time—which continues to this day—the public still views Houdini as a noble figure and a hero. The religious bigotry which he fathered still flourishes. A good example of this would be found on the popular television series "Ghost Whisperers." In one episode from 2010, series five, "Old Sins Cast Long Shadows," the character Madame Greta is typical. The writers of the episode depicted her in the stereotypical fashion of the average spiritualist medium straight out of Houdini's book. She was an evil fake who held séances only to cheat people out of large sums of money. She preyed on the bereaved who were desperately trying to contact their deceased loved ones. This caricature of a spiritualist medium, thanks to the popularity of these shows in the mass media, continues to feed into this theme by reinforcing it and remanufacturing it. This is the theme that Houdini made popular. If anyone had flung such an evil stereotype against Houdini and his religion, the world would have denounced them with catcalls of anti-Semitism. But use these slanders against spiritualism and they not only hold but thrive.

Another major accomplishment for which Houdini can take full credit is the decimation of the physical mediumship cadre that had flourished until his time. Mina Crandon set an example that took on Houdini and triumphed. Nevertheless, Houdini managed to vanquish her and trash her reputation. This example would discourage anyone from following down the same path as Crandon had. Mina Crandon was a woman who opened herself up to intrusive, grueling examinations of the scientific experts on a continuous basis for years—only for the public in the end to consider her with little regard, as no more than a common whore, despite all her sacrifices and courageous efforts. Certainly, the smears and slanders of Houdini were the only things that stuck to her reputation—and that of her husband, a medical doctor—among the non-spiritualists. She died an alcoholic before her time at age fifty-three, a woman broken in both health and spirit. Why would anyone want to subject themselves to the same treatment?

On the issue of fraud and trickery, in the case of the test mediums, the common complaint among all was the great expenditure of energy it took to create physical phenomena. It took a toll on their bodies to bring through other spirits. Many of the mediums were not always up to the demands and resorted to shortcuts, rationalizing that the ends justified the means. The spread of the new religion created a euphoria that made them push themselves beyond their limits. They were not always up to producing phenomena on demand, but nevertheless were always under an enormous amount of psychological pressure to do so. The more famous the medium, the greater the pressure. So some resorted to trickery to get them by. Once someone admitted to fraud, even just a single instance of it, the sum and entirety of their life's work as a medium was written off. This started with the very first of the modern mediums. Margaret Fox was once in desperate need of money and accepted a reward from a newspaper to denounce mediumship in general and confess to it being all fraud. She did so, but later tried to reestablish herself as a medium. Her followers never accepted or trusted her again, and she died penniless and was buried in a pauper's grave. This kind of thing happened to the great pioneers but never happened to Houdini. Once he was caught trying to sabotage Mina Crandon's séance, he should have lost his reputation and standing with the public. The sum of his life's efforts should have gone down the drain as well for his malicious crime. But not so. Instead, the word "whitewash" and the phrase "sweeping under the rug" are the best descriptions of what happened in the press. The double standard still applies today.

So, thanks to Houdini, physical mediumship vanished from the scene. Today's mediumship is exclusively mental mediumship, with rare exceptions. Today's mediums give messages from spirits and recruit their modern-day coreligionists through evidentiary information that they provide. These messages are of a kind where the mediums bring forth information that only the sitter and the deceased share. This proves the continuity of life from which the religion is based, so it provides proof of the religion not just belief. Mediumship negates the need for dogmas and creeds based on faith. Why do you need faith when you have proof? Mental mediumship appears to keep the fires of the religion going while not involving or threatening the health and safety of the medium.

But the results of the new, improved, safe form of mediumship have not stemmed the tide of the collapse of the religion's popularity. Today, those who feel the need to reach out to the spirit world seek the services of freelance psychics, of which there are many thousands. The concept of the New Age, which they inherited from the spiritualists, they have now hijacked for themselves. The protections from prosecution of the law which the spiritualists fought for, organized for, and won the rights for in law are now also the free entitlement of the freelancers who feel no obligation whatsoever to buttress the old religion. Cut them a check, perhaps? Heck no! So, while the old spiritualist organizations struggle to stay afloat with an uncertain future, the pop culture psychics reap all the rewards from the entitlement harvest. Gone is the standing-room-only popularity of the old spiritualist camps. Most are just struggling to stay financially viable. The idea and brilliance of a religion founded on proof—not just faith—falls further into the obscure past while the self-destructive culture of the opportunist marches on. Why go through the laborious task of mining for gold when there is so much cheap tinsel about? New Age freelance psychics backed up by the flashy, slick productions of the Hollywood mass media dominate the scene. They are either ignorant of their roots, or worse, spit upon those roots and the remnants of spiritualism. Those freelancers who join the movement to gain legitimacy and notoriety for their own practices seem to be constantly at odds with the religion. Many wear the spiritualist hat among many others—different "modalities," as they call them.

But one may ask: how did a grassroots movement as popular as modern spiritualism—a movement that swept across the United States and other parts of the world—unwind so rapidly and completely after such a promising start? We know about Houdini, the public interface and instrument of the unwinding. But what do we know of the stimulus that launched Houdini? On the one hand we have a talented, popular magician who got along with the spiritualists for decades. And then, suddenly, we see a metamorphosis happen as the gentlemanly showman turns into a menacing crusader against a movement where he even once had friends. This happens with the rapidity of one flipping a switch on a radio, breaking the silence with noise.

There are two possible avenues in which we may find the answers. The first was an old one that traced back to Sir Arthur Conan

Doyle. In correspondences to Dr. Le Roi Crandon, Doyle suggests that the Vatican recruited Houdini for the mission of taking down spiritualism and that Houdini's Catholic wife somehow pressured him into it.

The second possible answer to who or what stimulated Houdini to take up the mission is of more recent origin. The 2006 book *The Secret Life of Houdini* by William Kalush and Larry Sloman documents the fact that, along with Houdini being the international superstar that he was, he was also an international spy who regularly acted as an international counterintelligence agent and was thoroughly used to performing acts of espionage.

If we put these two items together, we can take the story to the next level. Hence, we have a theoretical basis for this current work of fiction. It is not the purpose of this book to insult the feelings of any admirers of Houdini, Catholicism, Judaism, or any other entity that might take offense at this book's contents. The purpose of this book is to entertain and put forth a supposition to a question that may forever plague history. That question is: what happened to modern spiritualism?

Chapter 1

Problems That Need Solutions

Monseigneur Giuseppe Roncollo, of the Office of the Special Committee on American Religion (SCAR), a secret committee answering only to the pope, sat at his desk at the Vatican with a terribly anxious look on his face as he addressed one of his fellows.

"I am worried, worried sick!" he exclaimed. "This news is very disturbing!"

"What's wrong, Monseigneur?" asked Father Alfonso Rossi, secretary to the Congregation for the Doctrine of the Faith in the Vatican.

"This woman in America, her organization, her new book, it's a disaster! She has a dagger pointed straight at our heart!"

"Giuseppe, please! What are you talking about?"

"I am talking about the woman, Cora Richmond, in America, her book and her new organization. They incorporated as a formal religion back in 1893, in America. They are very dangerous. You remember what has happened before? We almost lost America!"

"Giuseppe, you forget I do not work on the same subjects you do. I have no idea what you are talking about."

"Father Rossi, have you ever been to America? No? Do you have any idea how important it is to the future of the church? The money? The resources? Can you not see that they have turned the war against Germany by the sheer power of their industrial might and unlimited manpower? We cannot play games here, Father Rossi. This is deadly serious. I want you to understand."

"Giuseppe, I do understand that. What I don't understand is about this woman. I never studied her or her new cult. You must educate me."

"Very well, Father Rossi. If you have the time, I can explain it to you. She is the latest in these people from America who have called themselves *spiritualists*. They came about in the middle of the last century, and their popularity spread like a brush fire that consumed almost the entire country. They believe in direct communication with the dead. At the time of their civil war, they had even taken over the White House. Their President Lincoln had regular meetings with them, *séances*, where he got all kinds of information from the spirit world on how to manage the country and fight the war. He even had his top generals come in to plan strategy and tactics. They got detailed information regarding battle plans from spiritualist mediums. Lincoln himself and his wife were secret spiritualists. We have thorough documentation on this. Whether or not they would have ever revealed this to the public, we of course will never know as a result of his demise."

"What active measures did we take to stop the movement?" asked Father Rossi.

"As usual, our preachers from the pulpits had little impact. These Americans are very stiff-necked and independent, and that is why this office exists and why we must consistently monitor them. We contacted some of our agents over there, but the clumsy oafs kept botching the job. They followed one of the Fox sisters, leaders of the movement, firing pistols at her when they thought they had a shot, and of course they missed. The attempt only generated more sympathy and brought more people to the cause. The Fox sisters eventually died of alcoholism. But the movement they spawned just grew larger and larger until they had taken over the White House itself, during Lincoln's presidency. That's when we started complaining to our international friends about the threat. Shortly afterward they eliminated that threat. The successors to Lincoln went back to normal activities in the White House—no more séances. Although I suspect it was not for religious reasons that Lincoln was nullified, but for monetary reasons. Anyhow, none of our agents were adept enough to carry out this elimination. It was due to agents of a much more professional and efficient class."

"But, Monseigneur, what exactly is it about this new cult that is a threat to our religion? Do they deny Christ? The patriarchs of the Bible? Are they astrotheologists?"

"Well, you see, Father Rossi, that is the problem. In her book, this woman Richmond does not expressly deny the Bible. She writes her own version of the Bible and the cosmos that is entirely logical as it is mystical. Christ, the patriarchs, and their existence or nonexistence, she does not address. She lumps the whole period together and calls it one of the 'dispensations,' twelve in number, which wax and wane their way through history. So nothing is permanent. There are no chosen people. Christ is not the king of the universe or the only son of God. He is but one of the many messiahs, if he existed at all.

"What we don't want, Father Rossi, is another wave of spiritualism in America. We barely contained the last one. Now, with this new organization armed with their own bible, we could be on the verge of a much more highly organized attack on our religious hegemony in the New World. This means loss of enormous amounts of money and resources which we cannot get anywhere else. And America has been the richest source of new wealth and power for us in our efforts to dominate the world. We can't afford to lose it. The Holy Father will not be happy with us. He is completely committed to the Great Work and reaching across the barriers of other power centers to bring about a one-world society with its global government and single religion. This society will manifest the goal of the church—complete spiritual control over the peoples of the world. There is no control over the masses possible with this world of the spiritualists who preach individuality and teach people how to tap into the power of the spirit world directly. Whoever controls the spirit of the people controls the world. We must suppress and destroy this movement. We cannot coexist with these spiritual usurpers. They are anarchists who take away the loyalties of people whose families we have spiritually owned for centuries. This movement we must annihilate now, once and for all!"

"But how are we going to do that? Are you sure these people are that much of a threat to the Great Work?"

"I am afraid we will have to approach our international friends. Crusades we can do. Inquisitions we can do. But espionage we can never seem to do. It's too subtle. We are not so good at waging war through deception. Christians make inept agents. They fumble and bumble and don't get the job done. We are not as good as we used to be at social engineering either. We are prisoners of our old successes from centuries ago. Our dogmas and creeds handcuff us in this modern era. What we need are agents who are more adept at mythmaking and shaping the culture in order to fulfill our dreams of the Great Work and a world united under one temporal leader and one pope. This has been our ancient design. In the past we could only gain mastery over a nation's guilt. A people's dreams we were never able to fulfill. We seemed to thrive only in scarcity and dark times. Things like freedom and prosperity we have not been able to deal with very well. For the modern era, we need to partner with a different class of controllers—those with a more skilled hand in these times to wipe out this infestation of independent spiritual-usurping heretics who have no love for the Holy Father. And yes, these people are a real threat, Father Rossi, and I will tell you why, if you are not already convinced: because they would take the spiritual power out of our hands and place it in the hands of individuals and groups over whom we have no control, people who despise us. If their mediums can give them the information they need to live their lives, information from beyond this world, from the spirit world, then what need do they have of us? If the people of this world realize that they can empower themselves without us, then they will flee from our control in droves, and the whole structure of our existence will come down around us. We must take it upon ourselves to reach out to our international friends and subcontract this job out to them. That way it will get done efficiently, and we won't have to get our hands dirty with scandal because our agents aren't capable of doing the job, as we know from bitter past experience."

"What about the Holy Father? Are you going to present all this to him?"

"That I don't know yet."

"But you must. If it is as important as you say, you need his go-ahead—I insist."

"It hasn't been done before on this subject, but perhaps you are right. I wanted to keep him out of it. To involve His Holiness is a very grave step. I do have some discretion in this, but as you say, it does rise to the highest level of importance, so I guess it's too big a job for one man. Besides, I will probably need an express order from His Holiness if our international friends are to pay the proper amount of attention to this problem. Without orders, they may not give me the time of day. And I can't be caught in a lie with them if I tell them I have His Holiness's approval and consent when I don't. Oh, for the old days! You could just declare a crusade and offer indulgences for the remittance of sin, and you would have a vast army at your hands for wave after wave of holy war. No one would dare stand against us in those days. Now it's all about intrigue and war by deception. One group consults another secret group who in turn order their agents, all professionals of the highest order, into clandestine warfare. It's all nuanced and dishonest. It makes me sick to think that Christ's church must sink to such low levels in order to survive."

"Monseigneur, there have been many cults that have sprung up in America. Most end up failing on their own after a time. I am not an expert on this subject as you are. But are you certain that you are justified in your fears about this cult?"

"Father, you see that large stack over there in that corner that I have watched grow day by day. Several years ago, when I first assumed this office and started monitoring the threats from America, I tasked the Order of the Jesuits in America to conduct surveillance and send back to me detailed reports of the activities of the spiritualists. I have hundreds of such reports. I know who they are, what they are doing, their churches and camps, their publishing houses, and their newspapers and the circulation of each. I know how the other cults, as you call them, have disbanded to join them, as if bubbling into one great crescendo of heresy. It is not lightly that I sound the alarm now. God knows that His Holiness has had more than enough on his mind with this terrible war tearing into the bowels of Christendom. But God also knows the sleepless nights I have gone through waiting for this war to end so that we may shift our focus to this new threat. And thank God this war is finally over now. We need to refocus on winning the peace and rebuilding Christendom worldwide. This wave of spiritualism has already washed up on European shores—especially in England. They have sent forth their apostles to our homelands with their displays of supernatural powers and have won many converts. And on that godforsaken isle of England, I can guarantee you that this very night thousands of séances are going on in hopes of hearing a word from soldiers lost in the war. We don't want that to continue or to spread. Thanks to you, I have made up my mind to approach His Holiness sometime in the next few weeks and get his approval on the next phase—active measures to eliminate this threat."

With that the monseigneur pushed two piles of reports closer together with his foot.

Chapter 2

Meeting With His Holiness Pope Benedict XV

The date was December 7, 1921. The place was the Apostolic Palace in the Vatican in the private study of Pope Benedict XV.

"Greetings Monseigneur," said the pope. "I have read the dossier that you sent over. It is most enlightening on a subject I have had little time to study. It appears that you have kept your thumb on the situation, and we are much grateful for this. What I am not sure about is the extent of the threat that you perceive. You document the predecessors of this current movement, this is to say the Shakers, the Quakers, and the free thinkers. Are you certain that this current movement will not fade away and become extinct on its own, like the others have?"

"Your Holiness," said the monseigneur, "thank you for taking the time out of your busy schedule, Christmastime and all, to see me on this urgent matter.

"First, I would not trouble his Holiness unless I thought that the gravity of this threat was an existential one for the church in America. When the first wave of this threat manifested in the 1850s it was a veritable earthquake. The claims of the spiritualists at the time of the American Civil War are not an exaggeration. A full one-third of the population of the North had become spiritualists, including President Lincoln and his family. Our agents and assets in America confirmed reports that Lincoln was conducting séances in the White House with spiritualist mediums who were providing him with not just entertainment, but detailed political, strategic, and tactical advice on how to conduct the war. Our reporters documented the fact that even Union field grade commanders were going to the White House with their maps, not just to brief the president on the situation of the battles, but to get detailed advice on how to fight those battles by so-called deep trance mediums. I have researched all the archives for this time period. You may or may not know this, but your predecessor, Pius IX, felt that the spiritualist movement was such a threat to the church growth program at the time that he signed on to the international active measures and their agents in America to eradicate the White House of this threat. There were indications that Lincoln was prone to publicly declaring himself, his family, and several high-ranking members in his government as spiritualists. Such a declaration might well have dealt a fatal blow to Pope Pius and his pro-growth program. As a result of the international intervention, the program flourished and more than doubled the Catholic population in the United States under his pontificate. The coup d'état against the American government at that time was also a major test of the strength and coordination of the shadow government on the Great Work that the father general of the Jesuits signed on to with our international allies. Our agents alone at that time were not up to the task of promoting or protecting the Great Work any more than they are today."

"But Monseigneur, are you not convinced that the threat is now neutralized? There doesn't seem to be any real substance to these people, these spiritualists. They have no holy book, no bible, no formal system of theology, no sacred scriptures to control the minds of their people. You say yourself that most of these mediums who work on the street level are charlatans with no abilities whatsoever. They are simple, unscrupulous people who take advantage of the bereaved to relieve them of their funds. How can such a movement based on such a flimsy foundation possibly be a threat? They have no ancient cathedrals, no holy places, no seminaries, convents, or cloisters. Monseigneur Roncollo, I am still not seeing this as you do."

"Your Holiness, please, I stake my life and my reputation on what I say. If I may be so bold, and I do beg your forgiveness for saying so, but despite your perceptions I see the movement as a threat of the first order. It has a very intricate belief system. This system is a greater threat to us than the heresy of Modernism. Modernism is a form of iconoclasm that tears down the building blocks of our faith. We can in some cases turn Modernism to our advantage if we skillfully manage it. Spiritualism, however, can not only be iconoclastic; it can replace our faith with an entirely new faith. And now with this second wave, it is taking root in Europe as well, thanks to the mass bereavement brought about by the war. A beloved author in England has already pledged his allegiance to this religion because of his desperation to communicate with a dead son and other family members who died in the war. He takes many people with him due to the power of his celebrity.

"Your Holiness, please, let me address your concerns one by one. First there are many, maybe even the majority of spiritualists, who are simply trying to find an excuse to take money from people. But don't let that fool you, your Holiness. There is a cadre of true believers behind these people. They believe with every breath of their physical bodies that they have the true religion. These elites are at the core of this movement. Moreover, your Holiness, they are in contact with the dead. They get guidance from the netherworld. We have our own mystics and sensitives who guide this church, and they do for their church too.

"Secondly, your Holiness, it is true, they do not have the ancient buildings and holy places as we do, but they are nevertheless an asymmetric threat. They don't need to maintain these encumbrances as we do. And they can burn through us as a brush fire can burn through a field of wheat. They have already done this once before in their first wave, which is a matter of historical record."

"Monseigneur, what makes you so sure there will be a second wave?"

"This leads me to my third point, your Holiness. You are mistaken when you say they have no holy book, no bible, no holy scriptures. They do have those. In my view, they will have a second wave because now they are more structured, more solidified. This new organization of theirs, The National Spiritualist Association, is led by very astute people. They have all the structures—legal, organizational, and spiritual—to give substance to an otherwise chaotic mass. They are led by a woman who has produced a spiritual book that is very much their bible. Moreover, it has many advantages over our Bible in that it is truly egalitarian, not based on irrational favoritism. There are no chosen people, not Jews, not Christians. The people of her book only advance through personal merit. All are equal under natural law. This has a great appeal, your Holiness."

"Do you have any passages from this book, Monseigneur? Who is the author and what is the name of this book?"

"Your Holiness, the name of the book is *Psychosophy*. Its author is one of the leaders of this new organization, a Mrs. Cora Richmond. She is a so-called deep trance medium. In my opinion, she is an authentic mystic because the way this book is written goes way beyond her limited education and background. Some of the information in the book also correlates to banned texts in our archives that the public has no access to. Most troublesome is that the book reaches out on a very personal level to the reader and makes them feel a part of it, like they have a stake in the overall cosmology. This book is highly dangerous, your Holiness. Our faith is based on the fear of eternal Heaven and Hell. That is the basis of our religion and the pillar of the state. In this book, that fear is nonexistent. So state and papal authority would cease to have legitimacy in such a system."

"That name, *Psychosophy*, is a strange name for a book of sacred knowledge, don't you think?"

"Unfortunately, your Holiness, its genius is in the straightforward and simple tone that it takes which makes it logical and understandable to the common person. There don't appear to be any sacred mysteries, everything is matter of fact. Let me give you a few examples. There is no Genesis story. Instead, there is a quite logical narrative. On page 31 of the book: 'At the creation of the universe, souls descend from the celestial world to become living beings in the physical world to animate the physical substance. They thus come from innocence or a potential state and progress to the fully unfolded state to become Angels.' You see, your Holiness, common people, the swinish masses, work their way up the spiritual ladder to become Angels through their own moral victories. Angels are not arbitrarily created by God as in our scriptures. The book also teaches a revolutionary concept of history. There is not just one messiah but twelve greater messiahs and numerous lesser ones. These messiahs are Archangels who appear at each of the twelve dispensations of God's grace on Earth, so in other words, there is really nothing special about the Lord, Jesus Christ. They would only acknowledge that he is but one of the twelve major messiahs. The book also indicates that with no beginning or end to the universe and time only a relative thing, all people will eventually work their way up through all levels: human, Angel, Archangel, and messiah. They will accomplish this through a type of reincarnation that Richmond calls 'spiritual embodiments.' This information is like suppressed texts in our archives. Therefore, I say it is very dangerous. In my opinion, these books need to be suppressed. All the stops need to come out to find the publishers and shut them down—threaten them, if need be. But we do not have the ability to carry out such work, your Holiness. Therefore, I humbly beg you to authorize an order to our international liaison. It is a clear and present danger to the Great Work. They need to understand that their agents must get to work swiftly to execute operations to eradicate or liquidate this threat which is a grave potential threat to all of us."

"Monseigneur, I must admit, the picture you have just painted deeply troubles us. It does sound to us that these texts, the new organized approach, and the great level of bereavement due to the war are a recipe for trouble now that we truly don't need. Very well, even though it is an awesome step for us to take, take it we shall. I will have the order drawn up along with a dossier which I task you to write. We shall send them off to our international contacts and explain that it is imperative to initiate these operations in defense of our agreement on the Great Work. Please write up your dossier, Monseigneur, and submit it to my personal secretary. When we make contact and have given our partners time enough to study the matter, we will send word to you. You will oversee directing our liaison to the international organization and its agents. God bless you, my son."

With that the monseigneur made the sign of the cross and departed. Once he left the Apostolic palace, he made a great sigh of relief, and a great look of satisfaction came over his face.

Chapter 3

Blumberg

It took just forty-eight hours for Monseigneur Roncollo to complete and submit his dossier to the papal secretary. He simply made a few modifications to the one he had submitted to get his meeting with the pope. Several weeks passed and the anticipation was getting to him, making him more irritable with each new report he received from his spy network in America. "Jesus, Joseph, and Mary," he would say, "Jesus, Joseph, and Mary!" Then, on Januar7, 1920, in popped Father Rossi in the early morning with a mild grin on his face, knowing that this would make his friend feel much better.

"Monseigneur, you have your meeting today. I just got word. You are to be at the archives building at noon."

"Thank you so much, Father Rossi!"

It was 9 a.m. on Saturday. The monseigneur decided to hurry over to the dining area for breakfast. After that he went back to his room to get washed and more formally dressed. At 11 a.m. he headed over to the conference area at the archives. The security detail left the room where he was to have his meeting unlocked. At 11:30 he sat and read a local newspaper. At exactly noon he heard a polite knock at the door.

"Come in, please."

A short man entered with a black brimmed hat and thick glasses. He took the hat off to reveal a balding head.

"Blumberg, is it you? Jesus, Joseph, and Mary. What are you doing here?"

"Of course, it is me. You were expecting Moses, perhaps?"

"No, it's just I never expected someone like you to be an international agent! I can't believe it!"

"So you just think that the friendly Yiddish bank courier whom you've known for years is as simple as he looks? That I have no brains in my head? *Oy vey!* I can't wait to play you in a game of chess! You Christians are all the same—naive as all get out. This job must be darned important for me to be ordered to blow my cover for you, my dear friend."

"I am sorry Blumberg, but I didn't mean to insult you in any way. I just thought you might be someone more fitting my expectations. You look about as much like an international counterintelligence agent as Father Rossi does."

"Well, I am sorry to disappoint you, but that is precisely the point. No one would ever suspect me of being anything other than an invisible pedestrian, a common man on the street, totally unworthy of attention. Now you get it."

"Okay, Blumberg," said the monseigneur, shaking his head.

"So alright, now let's get down to business. Since this request came directly from the pope himself, it went all the way to the top. First, we must understand a few things. Number one: this meeting has never taken place. Number two: anything said in this meeting is to be completely in the strongest possible terms off the record except to our respective bosses. No tittle-tattle with Father Rossi! Do you understand, Giuseppe?"

"Understood, Blumberg. That's why they call my office the 'Secret Office.'"

"Fine, now that is out of the way. Now, before I get into the particulars, I must tell you that my bosses think that this whole dossier of yours is completely crazy. If it weren't for the pope, they would have thrown it completely into the trash. All this concern about religion currently, who cares?! I can tell you that these mediums or whatever you want to call them would be completely welcome in any of our synagogues or lodges. We will invite them in with a smile and a handshake, we are that confident of ourselves. They pose no threat to us whatsoever. It is only in the interest of solidarity and fidelity to our agreement on the Great Work that we are going the full distance on this. My bosses have instructed me to tell you that they have come up with an operations plan that will totally derail this spiritualist movement in America to the point where it shall never, ever, have the hope of recovery to its former level. And we shall do this great feat without the shedding of a single drop of human blood—ours or theirs. Now, let me give you a second to say something."

"Sounds fantastic, Blumberg, but how?"

"For one thing, shedding blood is messy. We don't do it unless we absolutely must. Then we do it with great secrecy and efficiency. But as far as dealing with new religions, its child's play. We have been liquidating hostile religions for millennia and are experts at it. Now, in case you didn't already know, we own the American media and the press. We just need to get one of our hungry agent celebrities to go after this upstart group and hammer away at them in the press until they have a hard time trying to find a rock big enough to crawl under and hide from the public. And we have selected just the man. He is an experienced international counterintelligence agent. He has done work for the American Secret Service. He has done intelligence collecting missions for our organization during the war, and the war, I might say, has come out very much to our favor as a result of the work of our network of agents like him. He did some very important work for us in Russia before the war. He is a fellow mason and the son of a rabbi. We have no fear that he will have any sympathy with the target group whatsoever, once he gets orders. What's more is that he is broke right now due to his flashy lifestyle and needs lucrative employment. And to top things off, he is married to a Catholic. Any ideas on who he is?"

"I'm sorry, Blumberg. I don't follow American celebrities."

"Of course, you don't. I forget. You spend all your time in prayer in front of the statues, when you are not sorting through your intelligence reports. Well, I'll tell you who he is. He is Erik Weisz!"

"Erik who?"

"Ha, Ha, I got you there, old friend. It's Erik Weisz, otherwise known as the Great Houdini!"

"The magician? Incredible! He is part of the organization too?"

"Well, of course he is. Otherwise we wouldn't recommend him, you silly Giuseppe. Not only is he a member of the organization, but he is the best we can possibly select for this mission. He is the best we have. And we don't play games. We know him well. He will absolutely rip the heart out of your rival in America as a lion devours a gazelle. He is a lion of Juda, after all."

"Blumberg, I am so happy right now, I could kiss your balding head. You make me very happy. I knew the organization would not let us down! But I don't understand. How is one man—granted, a famous one—going to bring down a massive spiritual movement single-handed?"

"Don't worry, Giuseppe. He has already made elephants disappear. What's one more elephant? Ha ha! They will be no problem for him. Besides, he is a crusty old agent and is fearless. He will enlist a small army of detectives, and they will fan out and wreak havoc on the spiritualists wherever they go. And they will not stop until every group of mediums, both real and fraudulent, scatter for cover like rats scattering from someone turning on the light. All the time, Houdini will get more fame and commissions for his public performances as he goes. Have no fear, Giuseppe. This problem we have solved for you. And Houdini, showman that he is, will always protest that he is the great protector and defender of the public against this false religion. His heroic legacy will last for generations. Bye-bye, spiritualism!"

"Blumberg, we owe you a million thanks!" exclaimed the monseigneur.

"Don't mention it, Giuseppe! One day, perhaps after we are both dead and gone, the organization may ask an equal favor from you. This one is already recorded in the ledgers. By the way, how does his Holiness like the latest vintage sacramental wine we have been gifting him?"

"Oh yes, it is safe to say that not only does he use it at mass, but he prefers to dine with it also."

"Wonderful, that is a great compliment."

"How are things at the bank going, now that the war is over?"

"Well you know, Giuseppe, if more flows in than flows out, we are happy. But I am not allowed to talk business on the Sabbath. I must go now, my friend. If we need you, we will get in touch with you. But I don't think we will need to. The plan is in motion, and I don't see anything getting in the way. The next time you see me, I will be my regular self, Blumberg the bank courier. Until then my friend, *shalom*."

"Peace be with you, Blumberg. And once again, many thanks."

With that Blumberg put on his hat and headed out the door. The monseigneur slept that night, the best sleep he had slept in weeks—like a man saved from the horns of the devil himself.

Chapter 4

Sir Arthur

Sir Arthur Conan Doyle—veteran of the Boer War, skilled medical doctor, and author of the world-famous Sherlock Holmes mysteries—was in deep discussions with his friend Dr. Ellis Powell over questions of religion. In public, Dr. Powell talked about the similarities of spiritual phenomena of the New Testament and how the plethora of mediums were coming out of the closet as a result of the public displays of mediumship and lectures from the Apostles of the cult from America. In private, Dr. Powell had grave doubts about the authenticity of the New Testament and the cult of Christianity. But he was too afraid to reveal these doubts to anyone other than his most trusted friends. Sir Arthur was one of them. This is how Dr. Ellis would put it to Sir Arthur:

"Since it's Sunday, Sir Arthur, let's talk about religious myths. The biggest religious myth that I know of is a whopper. It is the Abrahamic religious tradition that encompasses half of the world religions. Let me go over the following historic facts and see what you think. All the great gods of ancient times—Horus, Attis, Tammuz, Krishna, Mithras, Dionysus, and Jesus—had near identical backgrounds. All were born of a virgin, born on the twenty-fifth of December, and were resurrected from the dead. Both Horus and Jesus had twelve disciples, had their birth signaled by a star in the east, were adored by three kings, began their ministry at age thirty, taught at age twelve, performed miracles, were crucified, and were dead for three days. Their stories are virtually the same. Dionysus and Jesus both turned water into wine, were called the "King of Kings" as well as the "Alpha" and "Omega." Mithras and Jesus, along with both performing miracles and being dead for three days, were worshipped as God on Sundays.

"Do you see a pattern developing here? How come all these alleged historical messiahs have almost identical stories? Any guesses? Well, the answer is that we can easily explain this repeating pattern if we introduce the mating of astronomy with theology, thereby getting astrotheology.

"The star of the East is the star Sirius, which is the brightest star in the sky. It lines up each year on December 24 with the three stars on Orion's belt, or the three kings. The constellation overhead at that time is the constellation Virgo, the virgin. Therefore, they all appear to be born of a virgin. The sun reaches its lowest point on December 22 and stays dormant for three days until December 25 when it again rises in the sky. Therefore, the messiahs die for three days and then rise again on the third day. But the resurrection is not celebrated until Easter or the spring equinox because that's when the sun overpowers darkness and day becomes longer than night. Judas's thirty pieces of silver are the thirty days of the lunar month. The twelve disciples represent the twelve signs of the zodiac. The symbol of the cross is the cross of the zodiac: north, south, east, and west. Jesus's crown of thorns are the rays of the sun because he is the sun, or myth of the Sun God.

"You can go on with this, but I think you see the pattern. Today's Abrahamic religious tradition is a plagiarized version of the old Egyptian religion and the other ancient religions in between. There is even an original Egyptian obelisk that a pharaoh erected in the Egyptian city of Heliopolis in 2500 BC that the Romans took back to Rome, and now it sits in the center of Saint Peter's Square, and they now call it the Vatican Obelisk. Obelisks represent the rays of sunlight that beamed from the ancient Egyptian sun god, Horus.

"Given all of this information, and the fact that the Abrahamic religions of our world today are based on anthropomorphic myths—which, in reality, are allegories of the placement of the heavenly bodies—then why are the nations of the world still wasting their time fighting over who are the rightful heirs to the Abrahamic covenant?'

"So you see the problems that arise from humanity placing its faith in and believing in it myths. Mythmaking is the number one crime of humanity, and it is an existential threat to its survival. How much sense does it make to be fighting over the city of Jerusalem in an age when catastrophic weapons of war are plentiful? Natural law will not be mocked. Sooner or later, you play games with fire, you get burned. All of us found that out in our childhood. As spiritualists, we know that there is no reason for anyone to get burned. What we all need to do is embrace our moral responsibility to live according to nature's physical and spiritual laws. This means working hard, being honest in all your thoughts and dealings, being as good a person as you can, and living the best life that you can. We need to be people of the spiritual light, which is the light of truth according to all the laws of Infinite Intelligence. In this universe, there is no other way to live."

"Dr. Powell, thank you so much for sharing all of this with me. It really makes one wonder about the naivete of the generations that they can be so duped by secrets which are in plain sight out in the open. And they also are so prone to sell themselves short as to their own God-given powers of perception and sensitivity. And they are also prone to be led around by the Judas goats of this world into pointless religious warfare, all the while not knowing that they are all myths based on pinpoints of light in the sky. This is what we have to save humanity from, Dr. Powell—their own skepticism of themselves and their gullibility toward the man on a white horse who fills them with myths and mythmaking which are, in essence, lies and perversions of God's great creation."

"Sir Arthur, I'm an old man near the end of my journey here on this Earth. Soon I will be in the spirit world myself and will find the nature of things there firsthand. I must leave it up to a much renowned and energetic person as yourself to keep fighting this fight for truth for the human race in this world."

"I believe you will have some time yet here, but if I am wrong, then I hope you will always remember your good friend down here."

"I shall, Sir Arthur, I shall."

"Dr. Ellis, given what you have just so simply and clearly revealed, why have not rational thinking people dismissed these religions long ago as fraudulent? This is a great stain on human reason and the integrity and dignity of the human species."

"Yes, in an ideal world God's creation all have integrity and dignity, but the creation of human society is not God-created, but man-created. This is where we get in an extra layer of complexity. The people at the top must rule over the masses. They don't have the luxury of worrying about absolute truths. They do whatever they have to to survive and rule. So, if they must create myths and lies in order to rule over their wards, they do so. And the people don't give a care about absolute truth either in their everyday quest to survive. They believe whatever their masters tell them. If, at the end of the day they have food and shelter, they could care less about which of the gods they are told to worship. The Roman emperors were the best at it in ancient times. They created a cohesive culture based on bread and circuses for the masses to keep them docile to harsh military rule. If the individual cooperated, he had a lifetime of entertainment and a full belly to look forward to. If he resisted, he could look forward to prison and death. So what was the point for the average citizen to object to the official Roman religion for not being based in absolute truth? In time, the Roman gentry decided to exchange their old Greco-Roman system of religious myths for the Judeo-Christian system. Why did they do this?

"You have to remember that the ideal of Rome was to conquer and control the whole world. They looked at themselves as the heirs to the old Greek empire which under Alexander the Great had extended briefly all the way to India. But the Roman empire was a failure in this respect because it only controlled the Mediterranean—a far cry from the standard that Alexander had set. But what Alexander had achieved did not last long. It was a military phenomenon. What they needed to rule the world was a cultural phenomenon also to back up their military. That was the only way to harness complete control over a world society. This is where the idea of the 'Great Work' originated. It came from the old Roman gentry. They decided to chuck the Greco-Roman gods because they were too provincial and lacked the kind of global mandate from Heaven that was necessary to extend over the whole world. The Greco-Roman gods had no pedigree that the rest of the world could recognize or embrace as their own. They were not connected to the seasons or astrotheology. As a result, they were no good for the ambitions of Rome. The new horse that Rome found to ride was the body of Judeo-Christian myths. Abraham was a citizen of Ur in Sumeria. Sumeria had the reputation as being the cradle of all civilization. So now we have a patriarch who provides us with a pedigree. By connecting Rome to Sumeria, the Romans now have the ultimate legitimacy. They become the heirs of the first civilized society on Earth. They can continue to conquer the whole world based on the original Sumerian mandate of civilization. Their conquest is for the highest good for humanity to save it from barbarism and savagery. The Romans could claim this line of inheritance for the Great Work through Saint Paul, the Roman, who claimed the lineage of Abraham by saying that God had given it to the gentiles through the mystical death of the new son of God, Jesus. So there you have it. Rome now has the key to world conquest on a cultural level thanks to its usurpation. From then on, all the world's religions from ancient Sumeria to Egypt to Persia, and all the little ones in between, Rome could claim as hers. It was a brilliant stroke of statecraft and cost them nothing, simply exchanging one bit of lunatic myths and ravings for a more cosmopolitan version, but a version that you could use for a remanufacture of the old Rome into the new. Indeed, today we can say that the old Rome has now come back on the world with a vengeance and has colonized the world with its great power to spawn new Romes. Just look at the architecture of the Capitol of the United States with its obelisks, Greek temples, and Roman architecture. An old Roman from long ago would feel right at home. All roads still lead to Rome, even to this day. Rome never collapsed; it just transformed from a caterpillar into a butterfly and is very much with us. And the world is under its yoke in not just the military sense but in the cultural, religious, and most importantly, economic sense. This all stems from the Great Work plan of the old Roman gentry that was primarily the invention of the Pizzo family in ancient Rome."

"You mention the Great Work, Doctor, and I have heard that term before at lodge meetings. Is this the same Great Work that you are talking about?"

"Yes, it is exactly, even though only the highest levels in the lodge know this. The lodges are just one spoke of the great Roman system of world government. Another is the Catholic Church. Judaism is yet another. Islam is another. Bolshevism is another newcomer, an offshoot of Judaism. All these spokes, the top elite call 'Points of Light.' All of these reach out to control the masses everywhere on Earth. A more accurate phrase would be 'Points of Lies,' not 'Points of Light.' But you must remember we are not talking about truth but power and control. The higher self of the individual that yearns for freedom and truth we must sacrifice in order to preserve the bread and circuses society of ancient times. Nothing has changed in that respect. The Roman ruling philosophy of divide and conquer will never give that up as their objective. The masses are not to be liberated but are to be kept forever in the dark as to their higher purpose. They are to be sheep forever following Judas goats. They are to be drug addicts, indoctrinated and addicted to the bread and circuses lifestyle, forever. The elites need the masses for now to do their dirty work, fight their wars, and create their wealth. That's all they are good for until the elites can find somebody else. Until then, they need to stay ignorant and obedient. When you have such an ancient plan that has unfolded for generations and is so deeply entrenched in history and society, there is no room for plans to empower the individual, no matter how true or noble that pursuit may be."

"By God, Ellis, listening to you gives me the chills. So it's still the old bread and circuses today in the twentieth century? If we go along with the lies, they feed us and entertain us. If we resist the lies, we get imprisoned or killed."

"That is correct. Are you up for this fight, which you will ultimately lose in the end?"

"I have always fought for what is right or what I thought was right. I'm an old man now and loath to change. Since the deep despair I lived through with the loss of my son, I believe that God has awakened me to the truth about what it really means to be human. Humans, whether they know it or not, are primarily guided deep inside our souls by spirits of those who have gone before us. To be in touch with those voices is what it means to be truly human. This is because they who are on the other side are no longer tainted or corrupted by the material trappings of this world. It is here where we can find true wisdom. We can learn from their mistakes and not have to repeat those mistakes ourselves. The spirit world is like a deep well that is always there, bubbling up life, giving water in the form of wisdom. We can drink from that well or we can turn our faces away from it. That is our choice. Blindly taking orders from Earthbound megalomaniacs carrying out ancient evil agendas is not my idea of what it is to be authentically human. I don't plan on creating an agenda of my own to do battle with the ancient agenda. I just plan to give witness and testimony to the truth. If I and my friends have the freedom to give this testimony, I will not hesitate to do so. I don't see them throwing us into the Tower of London for conducting séances."

"I don't think they will feel the need to do that, my friend, given their total control over the many spokes of the wheel of our society. If you get too popular, however, they may attack you from a thousand different directions in a thousand different ways—ways and directions that you will never see."

"So be it, then. In a short time, I will have to face God myself, and I wish to face the Creator with clean hands and good works to my name."

"I don't think you will have any trouble, my friend. But just the same, let me give you an idea on how they will attack you. You are the most famous spiritualist in the world today, so it is you who they will make as a target. This new organization in America has come about as a remedy to all the chaos of the movement since the time of the Fox sisters. To organize and regulate for defense of the movement are necessities. But because they adhere to no formal dogma or creed, this will leave them open to infiltrators who will come into their ranks and weaken them with never-ending schisms. This will be in addition to the Points of Light groups, as I call them, that will have ample funding and will usurp the ideas of the spiritualist movement, corrupt those ideas, and constantly derail the movement until it becomes extinct. They will usurp the concept of the New Age, which is a spiritualist concept, and spin it in a hundred different directions. The ignorant masses will not follow the usurpations and will put all groups, the genuine and the counterfeit, into the same basket. They will condemn them all.

"First let me tell you about the schismatics. There is one such group that I have followed the progress of that I feel has transitioned from a schismatic group into a Points of Light group. I am afraid they are in the process of stoking another great war in Europe. As you have mentioned to me about your son and all the friends, we have lost in the war against the German empire, you must understand that this was all planned. There is one cardinal rule for the elites who run the Great Work. That rule is *no exceptionalism*. No one country or people can they allow to become too exceptional, or it will become a challenge to and will undermine the Great Work. The power of Napoleon was a threat to the system. When Napoleon crowned himself as the emperor, it was a direct threat to the system. He had to be brought down. Likewise, what Bismarck had created in Germany was too exceptional, too great a threat to the system. The Germans had to be brought down, like the French. But those who brought down the Germans did so at the eleventh hour. Germany is still too great a threat. Bismarck did too great of a job in building Germany, and even the Treaty of Versailles will fail to reign them in. But the global elites have no organic means to break the fighting spirit of the German people, so as it takes a dog to eat a dog, America will once again have to come in to sledgehammer the German people into submission. America is also an exceptional country with an exceptional people, which is why I suppose it became the birthplace of so natural and empowering a religion as spiritualism. America, because it is exceptional, they will bring down and destroy at a later time—probably early in the twenty-first century. In the meantime, the elites will employ it to destroy Germany utterly. This is the only way to move the Great Work forward.

"The Great Work elites throughout history are used to raising up another sword as the lady of the lake raised up Excalibur to smite their enemies. A Russian transplant to America—part of the spiritualist movement in New York state, the heart of spiritualism— has led a schismatic movement from spiritualism. For example, while the spiritualists maintain that all people have mediumistic abilities and can gather wisdom from the dead, this Madame Blavatsky says that only certain elite individuals, like herself, can do so. Moreover, the spiritualist guides she called 'Ascended Masters.' It is only they, certain special spirits on the other side, who have the psychic power strong enough to communicate with special individuals like herself. These masters brought her to Tibet. There they told her about the seven root races. The fifth root race, she asserted, were the 'Aryans.' It is the mission of the Aryans to bring back and restore the lost psychic abilities of humanity. The sign of the Aryans is the swastika, an ancient sun symbol. Certain philosophers in Germany have picked up this theory of hers and are claiming it for the people of Germany, saying that they are the modern-day Aryans. In the Great War, the soldiers in the field began to wear swastika pins and paint swastikas on their equipment. Occult society offshoots of Blavatsky's group have sprung up around Germany and are publishing their own works. You can bet, Sir Arthur, that the elite Great Workers will finance these groups to the hilt. They will finance the new Germany just like they financed the Bolsheviks. This is all a setup for the next great war. We can only pray that years from now, the ignorant masses will forget how it all came about and will not blame spiritualism for the schismatic groups or for giving birth to this monster in the making in Europe."

"Ellis, you mention this elite group, how do they do it? Who are they?"

"They are the great bankers. They are the elite families at the top who control all the money. They finance and control all wars and all peoples, because they control all money."

"You mean the Jewish families—Lord Rothchild?"

"No. Forget about the word 'Jew.' There are no Jews, just like there are no Christians. It's all just a word game. As I told you earlier, all the Abrahamic religions are fictions based on astrotheology. To call someone a Jew means nothing. To them, of course, it means all the mumbo jumbo that they have been brought up with. But those at the top are realists. They use the word 'Jew' as a tool to get whatever they want or need, just like the so-called Christians used the word 'Christian' to launch the Crusades and get control of the Middle East. All these designations are meaningless."

"So why do so many people believe in the Bible? Is it not their heart that tells them that it is true?"

"There are a lot of truisms and anecdotes in the Bible. But the Bible is just a creation of the Great Worker elites. It is their template. To that extent it is the truth. I can tell you that they have written their own future history in it. Jerusalem is to one day become the capital of the globalist state. But it will be controlled by Rome and its ten kings in the Book of Daniel. And its ruler will be a so-called Antichrist with '666' written on his forehead. All peoples will buy and sell only through his mark. In the Book of Ezekiel, they have predicted that America is the new Babylon and will someday be destroyed by a surprise attack from Russia. All these things are in that book, and they will finance these events into being because it is proof of the God-given legitimacy of their template. Anything that does not conform to the template, they will destroy. This includes, first and foremost, any exceptional people or nations that threaten the fulfillment of that template. Napoleon and Bismarck are not in the Bible. Therefore, they had to be destroyed. Likewise, the Fox sisters are not in the Bible. They had to be hounded to death and die penniless in paupers' graves in order to not threaten the template. Their movement is to receive the same treatment."

"Good lord, Ellis! What a diabolical, evil system!"

"I am not trying to discourage you, Sir Arthur, just trying to lay out the facts as I know them."

"Ellis, I am not discouraged. I still have faith that spirit is a higher power than these fiends. I believe that spirit and our loved ones in Heaven will not let us descend into permanent servitude to these monsters. Now you have gotten my blood up. You have given me more reason than ever to resist this nonsensical farce of a system that has the whole of the world under its thumb."

"Very well, but I just feel it is my duty to warn you what you are in for. As the most celebrated and famous spiritualist in the world today, you are setting yourself up for a public crucifixion."

"So be it. Let them do their worst. I swear on the grave of my son, I will not give in, Ellis. You will see."

"I'm afraid I will not see, my friend, for I have received messages from spirit that my time will be up soon. Therefore, I want to share what I have for you now. And I promise that when you do hear of my death, I will do my best from the spirit world to help you here in this one."

"I'm forever grateful to you for all this enlightenment you have shared."

"One last thing I want to share with you, Sir Arthur, before we conclude on this subject. All people, whether high or low, end up losers in this system. The elitist families who control everything with their money and their deception of the masses think that they can achieve the Great Work of the one-world society without ever having to take into consideration the laws of nature and the laws of God. The physical laws they respect because they must. But the moral and spiritual laws they flout and spit upon. This is the fatal flaw in their system. For any system to work correctly, all laws must be in balance. Because they respect certain laws and flout others, they are building a system out of balance which will one day come crashing down like their Tower of Babel.

"These puppet masters, although they wield enormous power and decide on the life and death of whole nations and societies and live in such opulence themselves while doing it, these people are the greatest of all losers. That is because they go to their graves with the blood of the masses on their hands. And the second they pass into spirit themselves they have no more power or wealth than the lowest pauper whom they have condemned to death. At that horrible moment they come to see the emptiness and evil that they indulged in during their lives. In the spirit world, all things are known. All moral failings the individual has to address. In the overall scheme of the universe, I would rather die a pauper with no blood on my hands, than an elite devoid of finery and power with nothing to contemplate but the pain and suffering I've inflicted on other people and were responsible for in this life."

"So, in the final analysis, Ellis, no promoters of this current system come out the winner."

"That's correct. We are all victims. What else can we expect from a system based on lies? We are heading for another Mycenaean Dark Age. Someday, all the systems of the world—the power and money of this world—will simply collapse. No system thus unbalanced can last forever. And nothing will be heard of again about this world. Without a moral basis to society, the carnage of our wars will increase exponentially due to the great advances in technology. We saw poison gas, the machine gun, and a hundred other advances in the killing techniques in the Great War. What will we see in the next one? Our killing technology is outstripping our moral capacity due to the unbalance that the elites have built into this corrupt system. At some point soon, the masterminds who run the Great Work will lose control. They are so arrogant that they think they will manage. They think they are like God. But until they bow to the moral and spiritual laws that are part of natural law, they are out of resonance with the rest of the universe. The system they have built is bound to fail. When their money system fails, they will resort to another general conflagration with a higher level of lethality worse than the one we have just experienced. The Great Work is a great trap for all. The future will not unfold as they have written down in their template. The survivors of this system after the final conflagration will want to build a new system very different from this failed hell. Spiritualism is a religion for the next society. It is too ahead of its time.

"So, all we can do now is to keep working in the positive vein. We must train our efforts on turning the face of humanity to the light of truth. We must put the emphasis on the moral and spiritual laws that need to come first ahead of the physical laws. They are the basis of all the other laws. The only hope for our human race and our beat-up old planet is to change its resonance to the love vibration of the universe. I know this makes me sound like a Pollyanna, but I simply don't know any other way to put it. Our elites with their Great Works plan of the ages make life much more complicated, difficult, and painful than it ever needs to be."

"I understand you, Ellis. My experience in the Boer War had always left me with the nagging feeling that there had to be a better way to do things. I will never forget some of the horrors I witnessed down there. Maybe people would be better off if they were just left alone and not forced to be a part of some grand system which they detest."

"Because America created the first natural law government, the powers that be did leave it alone to give it a chance to develop as they thought such a system would have the best chance for quick growth. But that system soon became too successful, too exceptional. So they knew at some point they would have to bring it back into conformance to the template. In the meantime, you had all these idiomatic religious movements spring up from nowhere. They were autonomous and potentially threatening to the current world religious systems—you had the Shakers, the Quakers, and the positive thinkers. Finally, you had the spiritualists. They were the most dangerous of all because they were the most autonomous. They didn't even express fealty to Jesus other than postulating that if such a one as he existed, then he was the world's greatest medium. How radical this was! Their popularity swept the nation and their missionaries spread all the way to these shores to include converts such as yourself. Can you imagine how much of a threat they are to the existing system if they go unchecked? I am 100 percent certain that plans are afoot now to attack and destroy this movement for good. They will use their best weapons. They will conduct this war by deception. I doubt that at any point the spiritualist movement will even know that an all-out war is being waged against them. It will all be clandestine and there will be no traces of wreckage to indicate that a war was ever fought. The identities of the assailants will be forever a mystery. It won't be like the clumsy efforts of the last century when the pope sent drunken Irish thugs out to take potshots at the mediums with their handheld pistols."

"Good lord, Ellis, how are we to protect ourselves?"

"Unfortunately, you can't. You can only trust that Infinite Intelligence will guide you. You will not know in your travels who is friend or foe. There will be those who greet you with the warmest of smiles who at the same time are conducting elaborate schemes of sabotage against you. You will not be able to tell who they are unless they tip their hand to you and make it obvious. But most likely, they will constantly lie and deny. They will tell you they are honest seekers of the truth while at the same time carry out their destructive agenda against you. That is how the game is going to play out."

"My time with you is up for today, old friend, I am sorry to say. I have tried to commit to memory everything you have told me. I feel like you have lifted my consciousness to its highest point possible for the moment. Please give my regards to all your like-minded friends whom I have not had the chance to talk to."

"I will, Sir Arthur. Until we meet again, best of luck!"

Chapter 5

Houdini

Born in Budapest, Hungary, a son of a Jewish rabbi, Erik Weisz immigrated to the United States in 1878. He read the autobiography of the French magician, Jean Eugéne Robert-Houdin, in 1890 and changed his name from Erik Weisz to Harry Houdini. In 1908 he wrote a book denouncing his mentor as a liar and a fraud. He kept his new name, however.

Houdini launched his career and became famous as a handcuff magician and stuntman. He also became famous as an aviator and appeared in silent movies. Above all, he did whatever necessary to promote himself. In order to get national and international contacts he did freelance spy work for the US Secret Service which was the CIA of its day. He was, in fact, an international intelligence operative who had many contacts and jobs overseas. Some of his missions were related to intelligence gathering in the Great War. His success as an international showman led to a great many copycat handcuff magician acts by others. Audiences grew tired of the more common tricks and demanded greater and greater acts of daring such as adding the drama of death by drowning. Houdini came up with ever more dangerous routines to keep his audience forever on edge. But at some point, the public had grown tired of even these exploits of the Handcuff King. Houdini's career as an international showman began to fade. This, along with his high living, put him on the verge of going broke.

It was at this time that the organization of the Great Work dropped in his lap the commission of a lifetime. With it they would springboard him into the heights of international stardom.

In the middle of February 1922, a courier had delivered a large dossier to Harry Houdini's apartment. This was an ops plan, or operations plan, for what turned out to be the crowning achievement to Houdini's career. He had orders to take down the religion of spiritualism. Such a mission was well suited to him. He already had a budding friendship with Sir Arthur Conan Doyle, world-renowned author and a celebrity among the spiritualists. Houdini had rubbed elbows with other mediums throughout the years. The ops plan called for him to make use of these contacts for a colossal publicity campaign. This would be all negative publicity aimed at the spiritualists to cause a nationwide—and then a worldwide— wave of skepticism that would inundate and then sink to the bottom those vessels of the spiritualist movement. Houdini was to meet up with his friend, Sir Arthur, make a list of all his contacts, and then with much fanfare and publicity denounce him as a liar and a fraud much in the same way he had done with his mentor Robert-Houdin. This was not to prove difficult. He was to use his stagecraft as well as his spycraft—both disciplines he had thoroughly mastered over the decades—to go on a grand tour, tricking, trapping, and publicly denouncing all mediums and spiritualists in the most vociferous and grandiose terms. He was to infiltrate every spiritualist church (for none were sacred) across the length and breadth of the country with his teams of hired investigators and private agents and track down and humiliate all mediums be they good, bad, or indifferent.

Even though Houdini had friendships among the mediums over the years, it was not difficult to turn on them given his new clandestine commission. It was like shooting fish in a barrel for him.

He always used to give the mediums the benefit of the doubt and accepted the possibility that what they were doing was real. Now, however, he took on the conceited attitude that if he, the Great Houdini, could not achieve mediumship, then no one alive could do it. Moreover, those who claim to do it must be deluded or liars. Not all the materializations and physical phenomena he had witnessed he could explain. Nevertheless, he found it easy to become King of the Skeptics and denounce all spiritualists as frauds. With his promotions offering large sums of cash for genuine demonstrations of mediumship, it was always easier to move the goalposts than it was to keep an accurate score. And as both judge and jury, he could never be satisfied that any example of mediumship met the criteria for authenticity which he had set. As a result, all such promotions he used as traps to humiliate and embarrass all comers and never lost a penny.

There was another character flaw in Houdini that handily fit his new mission of espionage and celebrity. It was his bias deep down as the result of being a rabbi's son. Spiritualism as a religion was an affront to mainstream established religion. It was an insult to his dead father, who was true to his Jewish religion. Houdini was not humble enough to be a rabbi himself, but he would not turn his back on the faith of his father, no matter what proof he came across. Even though publicly he always proclaimed his open-minded impartiality to the possibility of mediumship, privately, he had nothing but the foulest contempt for anyone who claimed supernatural powers outside of mainstream religion. To Houdini, they were usurpers and upstarts, all of them. Houdini cultivated his skepticism, which in the end knew no bounds. Ultimately, he concluded that there was no connection whatsoever possible between the living and the dead—there was none possible. But he never explored the basic contradiction that if there was no such connection possible, then there also would be no basis for belief in any of the mainstream religions either, seeing that they were all based on "miracles" or demonstrations of supernatural phenomena. If the spirit world existed, then Houdini had to see it on his own terms. It had to be presented to him personally on demand, much like Herod demanding to see Jesus perform miracles for him. Even in the Bible there is no example of a spirit kowtowing to such a high level of ego as this.

The ops plan revealed lists of contacts whom Houdini was to use in support of the mission. Among the agents and agencies he would use were not just private investigators and detectives, but publicists and newspaper people at every level who were to pave his way with the public. The bosses of reporters and editors ordered their workers to always portray Houdini in a positive light and make him the man on the white horse—noble, chivalrous, saving the ignorant common folk from the evil panhandling spiritualist charlatans who held the bereaved and the weak-willed hostage to their desires to contact their loved ones who had passed and were willing to part with their money as the mediums were willing to profit by this grief. The marching orders were to create a cult of personality around the magician that could reassure both pious and impious alike that God was still in His Heaven, and that only the established religions had the divine right to solicit funds for spirituality. Spiritualists were all frauds and illegitimate in Houdini's eyes, and so it would be with the public also once the press got to remanufacture the story. And much to the joyous relief of Father Rossi and Monseigneur Roncollo back in Rome, reports of Houdini's progress and the holy crusade began to trickle back to the Vatican both in the reports from their religious agents in the field and in the newspapers.

One by one, the press targeted and attacked the physical mediums all around the country. The machinery went into motion. Houdini was so pleased with himself and his new mission that he self-started a lot of it on his own, even without referencing the lists in the ops plan. Two months of furious activity commenced. Then in

April Houdini got a very important visitor. All the way from Rome, it was Blumberg.

"Mr. Houdini, I presume?"

"Yes, it is. I am honored by your visit. I got the message that you would be coming, and I have been beside myself with excitement."

"As they may or may not have told you, my name is Blumberg. I have come a great distance to formally brief you on this ops plan, mostly because I am most familiar with it, and I need to reassure people back in Rome that we are adhering to their wishes so that we can maintain their confidence. They are really the initiators and drivers of this thing. I have just got off the steamer so if you see me swaying from side to side, I assure you I am not drunk."

"I hope the journey was good. Did you get seasick?"

"Luckily, I only get seasick on small boats. But yes, the sea air did me much good. The Roman air is so dry, sometimes it irritates my sinuses. Before I say anything further, I must tell you that this meeting never took place. And what I say to you now will never be spoken of again by me and hopefully not by you either. Remember Houdini, it is by deception that we wage war, and our very existence depends on it."

"I understand this, Blumberg. And you can count on me to be silent on this and on everything the organization has commissioned me to do."

"Please, just call me Blumberg. That will do. The reason I am here is to see where your head is at with all this, your new mission. I must report back on whether you are up to this challenge or not. First, I must tell you what an important mission this is. The world rests on two pillars, Houdini: the government and religion. Both of those are fueled by financial power. Normally the financial power is not interested in either government or religion. Speaking as a banker, I can tell you that if we can make our money unmolested, then we care not a tinker's damn about either one. But ever since the modern era we have taken a special interest in the Great Work. You have been briefed on this before, so it says in your file. Let me just emphasize again how your mission pertains to all this. The Great Work has become a very complex organism with many players that together rule over the destiny of the whole planet and everyone on it. Those who knowingly or unknowingly interfere with the unfolding of the global plan, we must put out of business.

"Right now, the organization has identified spiritualism as a threat to the pillar of religion. It has become a threat and a problem because it empowers the individual and takes away from the group. If that happens, then you take spiritual authority away from those sacred institutions that the world grew up with—and that the legitimate powers that be control—and place that power in the hands of amateurs who have no such allegiance to us. We cannot tolerate exceptionalism of any kind in the international system. Exceptionalism in the world system equals chaos, and the world is too intricate for things that we have not planned for. Do you understand this, Houdini? We cannot accept anything other than established religions—no conjuring, no mediumship, no miracles outside of those of the priest or rabbi."

"I understand this, Blumberg, more than you know. I am the son of a rabbi, and as fellow Jews, we can look each other in the eye and know each other's soul. I have been competing with these spiritualists for years. You have done me a great service with this mission which I accept eagerly. It will be so simple for me to uncover their tricks. The difference between me and them is that I am honest about what I do. I tell people up front that it is an illusion and a trick. They claim their illusions come from the world of the dead, which you and I know is not possible. I hate these spiritualists, their inability to admit their fakery, and I relish the chance to cause their downfall. And I am grateful to have the unlimited resources of the organization behind me. As a matter of fact, I have already made contact with my own network as well as working the lists you have given me, and they have already started collecting negative information and some public exposures have already begun. The curtain is about to come down on their act.

"As far as religion goes, my father—the rabbi—always taught me that we Jews are the chosen people of God. To the seed of Abraham God promised dominion over the whole world. And if I, the Great Houdini, a seed of the chosen people, am not able to perform miracles from the spiritual realm, then no one can!"

"So you do not think anything of their gifts from the world of the dead? Are you not afraid of them?"

"Of course not! I am the Great Houdini, the greatest magician and illusionist ever in the history of the wide world. I don't believe that any of the so-called miracles of these spiritualist scum are real. And if they were real, then I could duplicate them entirely through natural means. I can do this, and all the time make them look like the cheats that they are. Just give me a stage big enough and I will shine the light on these snakes and their whole movement to the point where not a single place will there be for them to hide!"

"What a *mensch* you are, my friend, Houdini! I am just *kvelling*. You are a true lion of Abraham. If you do all that you say, you will save our world—the world of your ancestors—from one of the plagues of Egypt."

"Blumberg, to all others I would insist that they call me Houdini. But to you, my friend and fellow Jew, I would prefer that you call me by my real name: Erik."

"Very well, Erik. It is my pleasure to do so. I can see that our staff has picked wisely and that you are the right man for this most important job. They told me that they unanimously recommended you. I shall be happy to report that they hit a home run, as you Americans say, with you as the choice.

"Houdini, I know that you know your audience better than anyone. But I have sensed just now a bit more contempt—and may I say, hatred—in your tone for these spiritualists than I expected. I would advise you to go easy on the *chutzpah*, Erik. Remember, the public are like a vast flock of sheep. They are ignorant and gullible and have no idea what is good for them. Thank God for people like us to lead them. But nevertheless, the public is easily spooked. You are the best Judas goat that we have, but you must always appear open and evenhanded. Always say that you are waiting for the evidence and would consider a conversion, should that evidence appear. You must say this even if you aren't open to this. And you can never call them scum publicly, until the key to the slaughterhouse is safely in your pocket."

"Have no fear, Blumberg, I will make sure to make my true feelings stay deep within myself. And all the time, I will be the smiling, openhanded showman I always have been. You won't see me deviate until I have them right where I want them. Then I will annihilate them without mercy. You will see this. And it will be very lucrative for me personally. So not only will I save the world, but I will make a great living at it as well. But the real payoff is that it will please me to no end to humiliate these people into the dirt. I will feed my spite on them with every smile, every openhanded gesture, every handshake and false declaration of friendship. You will hear about it all wherever you happen to be. Just keep a supply of the latest newspapers."

"Very well, Erik. You have your briefing on the ops plan. You seem to be already working the plan and the lists and combining that with your own resources. I believe that they recommended you cultivate your friendship with Sir Arthur Conan Doyle to start and have him introduce you to his contacts in the movement."

"Yes, and all the while I assure you, I will feign simplicity and contend that I am but a simple seeker of the truth, open and amiable. I will look as pure and innocent as the lily but be the serpent underneath. I have had a healthy correspondence with Doyle for some time now. That fool considers me his friend. He thinks he can use me and my reputation to further his movement. He even thinks I am a medium myself. What a *schmuck*! I will build him up first, get his contacts, and then tear him down at my leisure. The *klutz* will never know what happened. Don't worry, the public will think of me as a true gentleman. And after I trash Doyle and his contacts, I will go to war with the real scum—the rank and file of the movement in all their little hokey hideouts and temples. Believe me, this will be the crowning glory of my career. None of these *putzes* will dare to stick their head out to do battle with the Great Houdini. I will scatter them to the four winds."

"Very well, Erik. My job is done here, much to the pleasure of my ears. You are a formidable foe and will make short work of this project, given your dynamic nature. I must be off now. I must depart for my journey back, and since you have made this an easy job for me, all I need is a ticket on the next steamer. Goodbye, Erik. May we meet again next year in Jerusalem."

"Next year in Jerusalem, Blumberg. Have a safe trip home!"

Chapter 6

Margery

So Houdini had his strategy all laid out in his head as to how he would accomplish his great mission and make his masters at the organization of the Great Work proud of him. His extreme vanity coupled with his extraordinary passion for publicity provided the psychological and spiritual fuel he needed to vanquish the array of spiritualists and mediums who would find themselves his target and the target of the enabling press. They would follow Houdini's exploits with vigor and fill their pages with fawning admiration of him.

Houdini would engage in public espionage as opposed to private espionage because spiritualism was a public phenomenon, even though he was highly skilled in the former. Although this is to be covered more in-depth in a later chapter, it was most convenient for the Great Work that Jews be employed in espionage. First, because of the tradition of official suppression of the Jewish religion and race in all Christian and Moslem countries in which they inhabited; the culture survived only in the shadows. They became a culture highly skilled in the art of deception and subterfuge as a way of life and survival. For this reason, they were natural spies and pioneers of modern counterintelligence and espionage. The greatest of these master spies, like Houdini and the Ace of Spies (Sidney Reilly, a.k.a. Grigory Rosenblum), would ditch their Jewish names and in a chameleon-like fashion assume Christian-sounding names that would provide them with cover in a Christian world. In this way the puppet masters for the organization of the Great Work used the Jews as the master technicians to do the dirty work that always needed to be done. They did this in much the same fashion as they used the Jews in the Middle Ages as the moneylenders and usurers to finance all the wars of Europe without having to dirty their tunics. Therefore, wherever you find the dirtiest of jobs of Western history, you will find the Jews. They are always tapped to perform those jobs. This is to keep the puppet masters safe, pure, and blameless. They always have a scapegoat if things should turn sour, which they frequently do. But it is not just the Jews that they use. All the world's cults they will feed into the furnace until they accomplish the Great Work. And what may one ask is the ultimate fulfillment of that work? It is nothing less than a one-world government, one-world religion, one-world economic complex all emanating from the one-world capital of the world, Jerusalem. This city is chosen not for its religious significance but for its physical proximity to all the power centers of the world. The religious aspect is only a cover to confuse fools who believe in fairy tales. The goal of the Great Work is the total enslavement of humanity in an iron coffin—a Hegelian master state in which they outlaw all individuality in the interests of the collective which the puppet masters control in perpetuity.

But back to the story: the main organization for the religion of spiritualism, The National Spiritualist Association was some thirty years old. It had as one of its main goals the sanctioning of fraudulent mediums among its ranks. It established schools and training programs and set legal standards of certification and credentialing. All of this meant absolutely nothing to Houdini. Deep down he considered all mediumship fraudulent and condemned the religion as not a "genuine" one. Such overt religious bigotry by a public figure was rare except in the case of the Native Americans. It is no coincidence that the Native Americans also believed in direct communication with the dead. This communication has always been condemned and forbidden in the so-called "genuine" religions that Houdini referred to. Anything that empowering to the individual, it stands to reason, is by nature antagonistic to the collective—something out of the grip of the societal authorities.

Houdini began to reach into his tool bag of espionage techniques and built up a machine that would conduct war against the spirits and their Earthly ambassadors. One such technique was his perpetual offering of large sums of money to any medium who could satisfy his criteria for mediumship. No one, of course, ever could. To anyone who could, such as in the case of Margery (Mina) Crandon, he could always raise some objection or other, and raise the bar of criteria on his whim. Thus he always came out declaring that no such thing as mediumship ever took place. At the Boston City Hall he provided a publicity stunt where he walked up the steps flashing ten thousand dollars' worth of stock as a reward in a very ostentatious display thereby tweaking the noses of all the local mediums. Nothing less than Houdini's demise would convince him of their power.

The subject that brought Houdini to frequent Boston was the internationally renowned Margery Crandon whose reputation as one of the best physical mediums in the world was acquired while abroad in 1923. She demonstrated phenomena to Sir Arthur Conan Doyle, and he made her known to Houdini in a naive attempt to convince the international spy and hidebound skeptic of the authenticity of the religion. At this time *Scientific American* magazine also turned to Doyle and asked for a recommendation on a good medium on which to conduct their investigation into the phenomena. He unhesitatingly recommended Margery Crandon to the editor. In November 1923, the preliminary sittings took place. In July 1924, the *Scientific American* committee accepted Margery Crandon as a candidate for a $2,500 prize that the magazine offered to the first person who could produce psychic manifestations according to scientific procedures of the committee. The committee consisted of a physicist, a college professor, and other notable men of science. The handcuff magician Houdini was a latecomer who pushed his way onto the committee in a classic display of audacity, even though he had no scientific qualifications. Margery Crandon had refused the monetary prize—being the wife of a prominent Boston physician, she had no need of the money. She never charged for any of her mediumship work. Her only interest was in spreading knowledge of the phenomena to an ignorant and superstitious world.

On July 23, 1924, Houdini made his entrance to the 10 Lime Street, Boston, address of the Crandon's and up into the séance room. He did this with one and only one purpose in mind—to debunk Margery and expose her as a fraud in the presence of the *Scientific American* committee, and therefore, to ruin her chances at any award or positive notoriety. He had no expectation whatsoever that when the series of séances were over, despite his best efforts, it would be he, the Great Houdini, who would be debunked. Unfortunately, due to the fog of confusion that Houdini created, the committee was dumbfounded as to what to do and therefore would not award the prize to Crandon. This was all that the press needed to hoist Houdini on their shoulders as the winner of the contest and promote him as the hero of the nation protecting it against the evil cult of spiritualists.

Margery had sat many times for the committee before Houdini finally showed up. They were favorably disposed to her mediumship abilities. Houdini, however, had bragged to his friends before he ever set foot onto Lime Street that he would expose Margery as a fraud. Such a high-level publicity opportunity for Houdini he simply could not fail to take advantage of.

At this point in the story, the reader needs to have a proper explanation of mediumship. The best mediums work through so-called guides or controls. These are spirits who have passed into the spirit world having once lived on Earth. For their own reasons they commit themselves to facilitate the production of evidence and phenomena of the world beyond to guide mortals in their struggles on this Earth. Margery's control was her dead brother Walter, who had passed some years before in a railroad accident. Houdini's embarrassment and failure in the presence of the committee during the séances he attended was a direct result of his extreme hubris and total skepticism at the notion that such a being as Walter could have existed. It was a hubris that would shortly cost him his life as he did not survive Walter's curse. The fact that Walter did humiliate Houdini did not humble him. On the contrary, it enraged him and stimulated him to become an even more committed menace to the religion. Spiritualism and Houdini became enmeshed in a death embrace in which both were to fall into the abyss as a result of the Crandon/Walter series of séances.

It was not enough for Houdini to be lauded and praised by the world as the greatest magician to ever have lived. But Houdini thought that every spiritualist medium was no different than he—illusionists all and potential competitors. He believed that all they accomplished was manifested using the same magicians' tricks that he had studied for a lifetime. It never occurred to him that anything else was possible. It never occurred to him that the true believers in spiritualism or its mediums had ever spent so much as a single afternoon studying magicians' tricks. He never considered it. The true believers of the religion spent all their time practicing and promoting it, and they would never consider wasting their time doing that. The fraudsters, of course, would. But being in the presence of the Crandons or Sir Arthur Conan Doyle you were in the presence of the true believers. This was Houdini's fatal flaw—his failure to accept this fact. The truth is that the true believers were not his rivals, his compatriots, or his students. Magicians and spiritualist mediums are a breed apart. They didn't understand him, and he didn't understand them. And it was Sir Arthur Conan Doyle's folly to fail to understand Houdini. He continually tried to win him over to his side, to befriend him, to trust him and to never accept that Houdini was a breed apart. Even when Houdini bitterly insulted and denounced Mrs. Doyle and her mediumship, not even that could stop Doyle from offering olive branches and an outstretched hand to his alleged friend.

The contrast between Margery and Houdini accentuated the fact that magician and medium were a breed apart. While Houdini raked in enormous sums of money for his performances, Margery never accepted a penny for any of her séances. While Houdini's demeanor was always serious and intense, Margery's was always fun-loving and full of laughter. While Houdini was a true believer in promoting fakery as fact, Margery was a believer in promoting facts beyond the fakery of this life.

The critical séances with Houdini happened in Boston in late July 1924. After fifty séances that Margery had performed for the committee, in which it had formed a favorable opinion of her mediumship, Houdini stepped in to try and undo all of Margery's work. After the first séance he witnessed, he boasted to the other committee members, "Well, gentlemen, I've got her. All fraud, every bit of it. One more sitting and I will be able to expose every bit of it." It is important to note here that Houdini did not back up his vain boast with immediate action, which was his standard procedure with lesser-known mediums. The reality behind the boast was that Houdini was faltering and not sure of himself. He was unsure of the trumpet for one thing, and other phenomena that he was unwilling to discuss. But this did not stop his determination.

Houdini later theorized and rationalized away all the phenomena his pamphlet exposed on the séances. He explained everything that Margery produced as a result of her being a clever contortionist able to contort her limbs to extremes that made her able to ring bells, produce lights, and make physical objects fly through the air—all without leaving her seat. She was a ventriloquist able to speak in low tones and laugh in feminine tones simultaneously. For Houdini's hyper-skeptical mind, this was the only explanation possible. But he failed to expose any of the phenomena as fraud like he had so many lessers, even while sitting next to her, holding her hand. He was not confident enough. So he came up with a ridiculous contraption that he surmised would make Margery's performance impossible. He would construct a wooden box, place the medium in it, and completely encase her so she would scarcely be able to move. It resembled the stocks that prisoners were put in during medieval and old colonial times. It immobilized the neck and arms. The box had eight separate locks—Houdini was so obsessed with locks— with three holes only, for Margery's head and her two arms. And as Conan Doyle later remarked, it was beefy enough to contain a gorilla rather than a petite woman. But Houdini was desperate at this point to change the mind of the committee judges and decided he had to risk all in an exuberant blitz of misdirection and obfuscation. After all, these men were eggheads and knew nothing about illusion. He should be able to plant doubts in their minds. First, he had to shut down the medium's phenomena, and this was the best way, so he thought. The stakes couldn't be higher. All of America was watching, and Houdini's reputation was riding on it. He had to come out the victor by hook or by crook, and he knew it. He was clearly out of his league now and had to find a way back to familiarity and safety, back to his scorched-earth tactics on the small-timers. They were easy marks, whereas this was quickly turning into a disaster. Houdini had written extensively by now, sending letters far and wide that documented his boasting and his protestations that all spiritualism was a fraud. If now he had to eat all those words, he would choke to death, so to speak, and become the laughingstock of the whole world and be its master fool, not its master showman. This is something that the vain, conceited ego of Houdini could not suffer. If this medium Margery upstaged him now, all would be lost.

So on he went with this last effort to sabotage Margery. In late

August, he sent his contraption up to Boston from New York. He first hoped it would intimidate the medium and she would refuse to sit in it. Then he would win all by default. But unfortunately, she didn't refuse but accepted the challenge. It made no difference to her. She knew the phenomena would come through anyway, regardless of what she sat in. She agreed to the strip search also. This was becoming a tradition among the world-class mediums now—the strip search. It started with the first mediums, the Fox sisters, and had carried on to its third generation in Margery Crandon. The skeptics have always thought it possible for the medium to store something in a bodily orifice that they could use to produce physical phenomena.

When the time came for the first of the boxed séances, problems arose immediately. After Margery was firmly locked in and the séance commenced, the entire front of the device burst open. Houdini rationalized that it was due to Margery's athleticism that she was able to break through the hasps and locks using brute force, even though she was in fact a slight, petite woman of no great physical stature. Houdini remedied the situation by adding more locks. But this was just the beginning of Houdini's troubles. Walter had complained to one of the committee members that Houdini had sabotaged the bell box. This was a box with a wooden flap that every time it was pushed down would connect an electrical circuit to ring a bell. This box was out of the reach of Margery locked up in her box. Walter instructed the committee member Comstock to examine the box in the light, which he did, only to find a pencil eraser had been wedged in the joint to make the circuit connection extraordinarily difficult, if not impossible. Houdini, master magician, who himself was not locked up in a box, denied any knowledge of how the eraser might have gotten there.

The next nights in the series of séances were even more tumultuous. After Houdini reinforced his box to withstand the superhuman strength of Margery, she assumed her place in it. The lights went out and the séance commenced. Suddenly, Walter accused Houdini of placing a folding ruler into the box. The committee members ordered the lights to be turned back on, and indeed, they found the folding ruler. This was obviously a setup. All that had to happen was for the bell box to sound once during the séance and then Houdini could demand a search of the box. He would then declare that somehow Margery had smuggled the ruler and that was how she had made the bell box sound off. And then the cardinal rule could kick in, namely that once a medium got caught in a fraud, that meant that her whole life's work as a medium was a fraud. Houdini would thus have his open-and-shut case that he could present in complete victory to the anxiously awaiting world. But as it turned out, with the unexpected announcement by Walter, Houdini got caught by surprise. The finger of guilt appeared to be at the doorstep of Houdini and his assistant Collins as they had custody of the box before Margery took her place in it. Witnesses said that Houdini was speechless and overcome.

But in hindsight, the more significant event for Houdini was Walter's curse. It went as follows: "You won't live forever, Houdini, you've got to die. I put a curse on you now that will follow you every day for the rest of your short life. Now get the Hell out of here and don't you ever come back …"

Walter never did appear again to any séance where Houdini was present. It wasn't until February of the next year that the *Scientific American* committee issued their decision on Margery's mediumship and rejected her claim to the prize. But it was only Houdini who denounced her as a fraud. The others were so confused by all the unscientific theatrics and simply said that the medium had failed to produce enough evidence for scientific certainty. But that declaration was enough for Houdini and his cohorts in the press to declare a victory, shallow as it was. So, from that point on, the downward mutual death spiral of Houdini and the spiritualists continued and accelerated. Houdini unleashed his private network of espionage agents that infiltrated many of the spiritualist churches across the United States and Canada as they moved the war into high gear. The network started the practice of not just detecting fraud but then turning the fraudsters over to the police for prosecution.

But this was not enough for Houdini. As previously written, Houdini did not differentiate between good mediums and bad, between fraudsters and true believers. Instead he declared all mediumship and the entire religion to be bad and worthy of only one fate—complete death. Both Walter and Houdini had identical plans for each other. So, in 1926, Houdini advocated the banning of the religion altogether to the United States Congress. He gave testimony on proposed legislation that would outlaw mediumship or "pretending to unite the separated." The secretary of the board of the National Spiritualist Association denounced Houdini as "a pronounced atheist and infidel." The public hearings on the legislation degenerated into endless charges and countercharges between spiritualists and agents of Houdini's anti-spiritualist network. Houdini's network finally lost the battle when one of their chief investigators, Rose Machenberg, made the charge that spiritualism had penetrated the upper echelons of the United States Government to include many senators and President Coolidge himself. After this disclosure, the debate came to an end and the legislation died in committee.

Houdini's anti-spiritualist campaign reached its peak in Chicago where he and his agents allegedly debunked over eighty mediums in an eight-week period.

Chapter 7

An Interview With Comyns Beaumont

The war between spiritualism and Harry Houdini ended abruptly on Halloween, (All Souls Day in the Catholic calendar), October 31, 1926, at Sinai Grace Hospital in Detroit, Michigan. Houdini at age fifty-three, in the prime of his life, died in a mysterious fashion of a ruptured appendix. One doctor speculated that he had died of traumatic appendicitis brought on by punches to the stomach from a man who had been testing Houdini's abdominal muscles. But such a case is so rare as to have been thought impossible. The sudden death of Houdini caused a wave of shock and alarm across North America and overseas. There was hardly a spot in the Western world that wasn't intimately familiar with Harry Houdini and his work. The only people who did not appear to be surprised were his archenemies, the spiritualists, who had all heard of the events on Lyme Street in Boston and Walter's curse. They waited for its fulfillment.

But now that the war was over, the advocates of spiritualism had to deal with the wreckage left behind. They had to look to the future and move on. But the question for the moment was whether it could be possible to carry on as before. Spiritualism began in 1848 in a process of spontaneous combustion. Spirituality in America was not tightly regulated as in most parts of the world. There was no state religion. Although the country was nominally Christian, its forefathers were deists and freethinkers. They even got their ideas for culture and governance from observing the Native Americans whom they displaced. In this religious power vacuum dropped spiritualism. And like a spark that found its way onto dry tinder, it ignited into a movement that encompassed one-third of all the nation's religious believers shortly after the war between the states had ended. That war was a bloodbath that proved fertile ground for the growth of the religion. After this first wave came a second wave, this time spreading overseas, a product of the bloodbath of the Great War. But all the controversy that Houdini caused had cut that wave short. Spiritualism had lost its former momentum. It was up to those true believers who were left not just to find a way forward, but to analyze what had happened and what went wrong. This was a job for a detective—a Sherlock Holmes. Only a man who could come up with the profoundly complex plots of that detective could solve this problem. Although Houdini later portrayed his friend, Sir Arthur Conan Doyle, as an amiable dunce and a naive simpleton, Doyle possessed a sharp mind that had a knack for getting to the root causes of problems. That is what made his Sherlock Holmes mysteries so fascinating to the general public. So Doyle decided to put on his figurative double-billed Holmes hat, and with a lit pipe, follow the trail of one of the world's great mysteries.

In the back of his mind simmered his last meetings with his old friend, the late Ellis Powell. Those meetings were never far from his mind. The proof that Powell gave to him about the fraudulent nature of the world's great religions and their basis in astrotheology led him to thinking. And the most important thought he had was that such a powerful fraud overshadowing religion could only be perpetuated not by a single individual but by a network of very powerful individuals. It would have to be the most powerful group of conspirators ever to pull off such a massive fraud. The motive for the individual religions is simple. They all want to portray themselves as the most universal, one true religion thus making all the others evil heresy. They all want to depict themselves as worshiping the one true godhead and the true believers as the chosen race above all others. It doesn't matter where their basic ideas come from. All that matters is who has the means and the opportunity to pull off their worldwide conspiracy to capture the souls of all humanity.

To help answer this question, Doyle decided to contact an English acquaintance of his. He was a young Fleet Street reporter by the name of Comyns Beaumont. Doyle was aware from Powell before his passing that Beaumont had in his spare time undertaken a line of research that had opened a completely new avenue for looking at the problem of the great religions of the world. Doyle thought that this analysis might shed light on the current anti-spiritualism that Houdini had so successfully tapped into. Maybe this inquiry would answer the question of how a spiritual movement with its primary motive to empower and uplift the spiritual life of the masses could be so successfully attacked and left to flounder by a single man's irrational hatred.

Doyle and Beaumont decided it was more relaxing for them to meet at Doyle's house in East Sussex. There they both could leisurely discuss some rather heavy subjects. The young Beaumont was only too happy to help the famous creator of Sherlock Holmes. But Beaumont was the one to do most of the talking as it became obvious that he had a great deal to say, which Doyle was anxious to hear about.

"Good morning, lad. Can we get you some tea?" said Doyle.

"Yes, that would be splendid."

"So nice of you to break away from Fleet Street during the busy season."

"It's always the busy season down there, I'm afraid. Fleet Street never sleeps."

"Well then, some time in the peace and quiet should do you some good, I suspect."

"I'm very happy to be here with so great an author and thrilled to accept your kind invitation."

"Well, we have plenty of two things here: time and tea, so you make yourself at home. Now I would like to ask you about what got me on to this subject. My old dear friend Powell before he died gave me a thorough briefing on astrotheology and how they formed the basis of not just the Bible but all the world's great religions. This would lead one to conclude the fraudulent nature of all the biblical stories, and the fact that these tales are just creations and personifications of the positions of the planets and stars in the sky. My question to you, my lad, is who did this and why was it done? It seems a rather cynical way to handle the most sacred aspects of a person's spiritual existence. I consider it a crime for even one person, not to mention a whole society generation after generation, to be subject to these lies. It is an abominable evil, is it not?"

"Powell did have a thorough grasp of the problem of astrotheology and the fact that it was a giant hoax perpetrated on humanity for thousands of years all over the globe right up to the current time. But Powell only knew half of the story. We had talked some, but I never had the chance to fully explain my work to him. I have dedicated my work to exposing the other half of the story. The whole truth is that the Bible is not just based on astrotheology alone. Most of the biblical stories are in fact based on ancient events and personalities. But they did not occur where they were said to have occurred or by whom. Unfortunately, my theories are not as easy to exhibit as those of the astrotheologists. All you must do to make those understandable is to read from the Bible and then look up at the night sky to see what you just read. What I have found, however, takes some detailed study of the places referred to in the Bible. An extensive trip to the Middle East is also very helpful."

"Well, go ahead lad, and share with me what you have got so I can decide for myself what it is worth."

"Very well, then. Ellis Powell was always talking about the 'Great Work' and the super-secret organization that runs the whole world's events today from the deep shadows of power. I am also of that same conviction. I have seen more than enough evidence of this in my short lifetime. If you were to tell me in 1910 that Europe, a continent that ruled the world, would today be a second-rate power to America, I would not have thought it possible. But here we are. Does anybody know what happened and why? Something so strange happened that none of the crowned heads of Europe could figure it out. But whatever it was, it cost them their dynasties and, in some cases, their lives. They were puppets that shadowy puppet masters deep behind the scenes led into war. After the disaster was over no one could answer the question as to why it had happened. I think the kaiser may have gotten the closest to the answer when he blamed the Freemasons. He was referring to the secret society, the Black Hand, that produced the assassins who took the life of the archduke of Austria. But even this move in the right direction misses that mark. If you were to point to one group and say they run the organization of the Great Work, who would be that group? Is it the Catholics, the Jews, the Freemasons? Is it the Communists, the Socialists, the Moslems, the churches, the civic organizations, the banks, the corporations? And the answer in all cases is yes. It is all of them! They are all compartments of the same pyramid structure. They are compartmentalized to be kept in the dark as to the true relationship that exists among all the separate parts. As to who sits at the top of the pyramid and runs the whole machine, obviously the kaiser didn't—nor did the other great monarchs. This organization of the Great Work obviously had no further use for the Hohenzollern, Hapsburg, or Romanov dynasties as they have all vanished from the face of history in four short years. These were three of the most powerful families that ever lived. But the three together were not powerful enough to stop the will of the organization of the Great Work which swept them from the field. It took only one simple act of espionage by one of their shadowy groups to completely change history forever—breathtaking, is it not?"

"Absolutely, please have more tea and continue."

"My studies have all led me to one place. I trace the origins of this organization back to the Roman emperors. The Flavian emperors breathed life into this group and put it into motion. Emperor Constantine put on the finishing touches. It still exists today, much unchanged in purpose and power. The Roman emperors constructed this shadowy monstrosity because they wanted to gain immortality for themselves. They were all about raw power and wanted something that they designed to rule over the human race for all time as an extension of them. They designed this war machine like they did the Roman phalanx, except it would keep in perpetual motion and devour everything until it enslaved the entire human race in perpetual subservience until the end of time. The emperors, even though the people of Rome worshiped them as gods, knew that they would die. The machine that they created, however, they made to live on forever and give them the immortality that they craved. One day their creation would encompass the entire human race in a one-world global government in which all were slaves and lived to worship the state. This was the only situation that could make their immortality complete. If the human race existed, Roman power would exist, but not necessarily in Rome. Constantine made Constantinople his capital, and the ultimate world capital was to be the fake Jerusalem that Constantine built and adorned himself. And the plan still unfolds to this day. Nothing has changed. The age-old plan determines our daily events. The emperors took the art of manipulation and secrecy and turned it into a hard science. Ancient Rome had been their laboratory, and they were all masters of the game of power, stealth, and espionage. They determined history hundreds of years before it was made. They hide their plans in plain sight to convince themselves of their superiority over the ignorant herds of humanity. They know that if immorality prevails in human society, they shall prevail. Any movement such as your spiritualism which professes a higher morality they swat down as a person swats a mosquito that impertinently tries to get a free blood meal."

"My dear lad, can you tell me who these people are? Do I know them? I have met my share of famous people in my time due to the popularity of my books. Can you tell me who they are?"

"Sir Arthur, I am confident that you meet with their agents every day, but you don't know it. Indeed, you carried on a friendship with Houdini without knowing who he really was. There is your answer. You really can never tell who these people are because it would mean death to them. And ultimately all the rest of us are unwitting agents working for the Great Work. We all serve in the pyramid whether wittingly at the highest levels or unwittingly at the lower ones. The danger comes from chaps like you who threaten to turn that pyramid upside down—can't have that! You see why this is a lot harder to explain than Powell and his astrotheology theories? If you want proof of what he was talking about, all you must do is look up in the sky. The history of the West is the history of the organization of the Great Work. But finding the causal connections and tying them to names, dates, places, and times is like trying to resolve one murky mystery after another. This organization—the most powerful in the history of the world—exists in a mire, much like your Grimsby mire in your work, *Hound of the Baskervilles*. I can describe it with some generalities. First the organization, those at the top, I and others call the 'black nobility of Europe.' They were the powerful old families of Europe. In some cases, they can trace their lineages to the old imperial Roman emperors. They were the only people with the resources to propel the machinery of the organization forward through the centuries. And today they own the legal systems, the banking systems, the religious establishments, the international intelligence gathering networks, and last but not least, the press and the academic establishments. All is subservient to them. And above all, no exceptionalism of any kind will they allow. So any movement like your spiritualism, which tries to give spiritual power, the most critical form of power which everything else depends on, back to the people with no strings attached, they will squash. The black nobility are the kings and queens on the chessboard. They marry into new families and discard old ones. They sacrifice everything for the Great Work. All shall die, but the Great Work will live on to one day bring total glory to their ancient creators, the emperors of Rome. Anything or anyone that threatens the Great Work shall perish. And Sir Arthur, if the Hohenzollerns, Hapsburgs, and Romanovs were all expendable, then what chance do you and your group of spiritualists have of saving the world from itself? None, I dare say. And I don't say it with condescension. God knows, the world is overdue for a break from savagery. I salute you and your group, Sir Arthur, for your courageous and wholesome efforts."

"Thank you sincerely. You are most kind to say that. I'm still at a loss, however, as to how you and Powell were to find the connection to the Roman emperors in the grand conspiracy. What evidence pointed you in this direction?"

"It's a huge panorama and I was going to touch upon it soon. It both amuses and baffles me how we English fancy ourselves as biblical scholars of the highest order but can't recognize what is clearly staring us in the face. Along with every good English schoolboy, I studied the Bible to the point where I became intimately familiar with its places in my mind: Jerusalem, Babylon, Jericho, Caesarea, and the others. I also had vivid pictures in my mind of the people: the Egyptians, Jews, Greeks, Persians, and so on. But a funny thing happened when I reached manhood and made my way to the Middle East to see these places. In fact, I was thunderstruck and dumbfounded by my first visit."

"In what way?"

"Well, you see that none of the places were as I pictured them—and neither were the people. In my mind, I had constructed those places as the Bible has them written—grand cities with huge buildings and hanging gardens—the wonders of the world. I imagined the massive fortresses surrounded by great hills and mountains. There were raging waters with powerful sea swells that challenged huge ancient rowing galleys that were part of vast powerful opposing fleets. On the decks of those ships were tall, muscular, athletic warriors whose descendants still inhabit those lands on the Mediterranean today. But when I got to those epic places of the Bible, what did I see? Instead of the churning seas I saw flat water hardly able to move with not ever a tide worth mentioning. Instead of the ruins of once grand cities with their palaces, I saw nothing but desert and sand—nothing but sunbaked desert! No one could ever convince me that anything of any importance was ever there. How could a great city ever find the agricultural base to feed itself in such areas? I went to what is purported to be the biblical Babylon to see the hanging gardens and found not a trace of anything. How can the eighth wonder of the world leave not a trace on the land? And Babylon itself was nothing. Where could it be? All we see are a few bricks and rocks. The great Babylon of the Bible was never there. That's a lie, I am certain. And so it was with every place I went—flat, sand, desert, and nothing but rocks. The mountains of this land wouldn't even make a good hill in England. That pile of bricks over here, that was Jericho. That pile of rocks over there, that was Jerusalem. It occurred to me that this was all a huge hoax. In no way did the sunbaked dust and the piles of rocks resemble the lands of the Bible, nor could they ever. I began to document everything that I saw. And then I thought that the ruins of old sites in England that I had seen—like those of Edinburgh, York, and Dunbarton—more closely resembled what the Bible described, much more so than these sites. And then it dawned on me and started to make sense. The events and stories of the Bible did not take place over there at all. That was not possible in this godforsaken dust bowl. However, perhaps they did occur but somewhere else like in old Britain? And the more I investigated the matter, the more I found evidence for my hunch. Not only do the stories and descriptions of everything in the Bible fit like a hand in a glove in England, but the stories of the people fit also, those who conquered and subdued the land in grand fashion. The people who conquered and subdued the nations of Britain were none other than the Romans and their emperors. And the greatest of all emperors, and the one who created the organization of the Great Work in the form we now recognize it, was himself a Briton. It was Emperor Constantine.

"Oh, how it all started to fit—the hoax, the greatest deception in the history of the world. I had it all right in front of me. There are mountains of evidence, and it will take the rest of my young life to get it all properly documented and explained. It is a bigger story than Fleet Street could have ever hoped to uncover. You see, Sir Arthur, the Roman emperors created this hoax so it would facilitate their worldwide global conspiracy. The story that they concocted was that civilization started in the East and came to the West. The truth is the opposite. Civilization started in the West and worked its way East. All of the ceremonies, regalia, and rituals of the Catholic church the Romans plagiarized from the ancient druidic churches. And those who did not go along with the plagiarizing they executed. That was the Roman way, and still is."

"So you are saying that the Holy Land is not the Holy Land? You are saying that the Roman emperors wrote or rewrote the Bible so as to create this great conspiracy against humanity to enslave it, and that it is still going on today?"

"Yes, I am saying that exactly, and the conspiracy is in its final phases. There was some kind of worldwide cataclysm in the distant past. The Bible says it was a great flood. The predeluvian world had a lot less water on it and there was much more land. Somehow, many millennia ago, a comet or planet swept by the Earth bringing a great deal of water with it that created a deluge. The ancients wrote about the cataclysm and how it wiped out the Atlantean civilization. The remnant of Atlantis survived in Britain and Ireland. They were the only surviving civilization at the time of the reconstruction of the world after the great cataclysm. The history of the Old and New Testaments is the story of old Britain and Ireland. I have found enough evidence of this to fill volumes. The Bible was deliberately altered and important records relating to the history of Britain and Ireland were suppressed. The works of the Roman historian Tacitus were extensively rewritten to accommodate the new narrative with regards to the so-called Holy Land. This process started under the Flavian emperors and concluded with Emperor Constantine who put all the last finishing touches to it. Constantine salted the Middle Eastern desert with all sorts of fake relics and ruins to convince a naive European population of the legitimacy of the new Roman Christian civilization. So, while our friend Powell was correct about astrotheology being the basis for the Abrahamic religions, the history of Christianity was uprooted from ancient Britain by the Roman emperors and replanted in the deserts of the Middle East for their own purposes. This is what I call the 'Great Deception.' So the Great Work is based on this Great Deception. I have gathered all the evidence and now have started writing books on it. It should take me many years to finish. But I have found, among other things, that the history of Judea and Samaria is in fact the history of Northern and Southern Britain. This is painfully obvious to anyone who wants to start looking."

"This is all very fascinating, my boy, but can you give me some specifics to go on?"

"Absolutely. It's hard to know where to start but I can give you some examples. What you find is despite all the literature concerning the antiquity of many of the world's civilizations, there is no trace of high civilization in India before the seventh century BC. The same can be said for Greece. Historical Greece bursts into view with full evidence around 600 BC. Before that, the evidence is sparse and unimpressive. Heinrich Schlieman found a pile of ruins in Turkey and claimed it to be the city of Troy from Homer. But there is nothing convincing about the find. Indeed, if invaders attacked the place with a fleet of a thousand ships over a period of ten years you would expect to find a great city much greater in size than the paltry pile of rubble that Schlieman has discovered.

"Anthropologists are finding with more certainty that the myth that civilization started East and spread West is the greatest myth of all ancient history. At no time was there any migration from Asia into Europe. One point that I and others have noticed going back to the time of Henry VII is how closely the ancient Hebrew and Greek is to Welsh. Yet how can this be? The name David, for example, predates Hebrew. It is first found in the ancient tongue of the Welsh, the Cymric language. It was a popular name of the ancient Britons long before it appeared in Hebrew. And there are many other examples. How can it be possible for so many words to be common at opposite ends of the ancient world?

"We have the preposterous nature of the claims that the great locations of ancient times that changed the course of civilization were located in the vast dusty wastelands of the Middle Eastern deserts—such a notion is farcical. Look at the case of Caesarea. This was the alleged assembly area and support base of Titus's attack on the alleged Jerusalem. It was the most important civil and military center of the Roman army. Yet no trace of it is left to look at today of the once sprawling metropolis. A few ruins still exist from the crusades, but other than that, it has vanished completely. Josephus, the Roman historian, claimed that Caesarea existed on a tidal river and that the tides flushed the city drains in an extensive drainage system. There are only two problems with this statement from today's standpoint. The first is that no one has found any trace of this drainage system. The second and more significant problem is that the Eastern Mediterranean has no tides. So the place called

Caesarea today either never existed or existed somewhere else—a place with tides.

"On the other side of the ancient world, Britain, we have the mystery of the Macedonian coins. If a cache of Macedonian coins from the time of Phillip of Macedon appeared somewhere in British ruins, then that would be a strange puzzle as to how they got there. You could easily rationalize it as a onetime event from some wayward travelers from Greece who got lost and somehow ended way up in Britain. But this is not the case at all. We find Macedonian coinage all over Britain and Ireland, just as if it were the coin of the realm. How can that possibly be? How could this druidic backwater of pre-Roman times possibly have used Macedonian coinage as its standard form of currency when the alleged Macedonia was on the opposite end of Europe?

"Then we have the case of the ancient symbol and national emblem of the Macedonians: the unicorn. The prophet Daniel described Macedonia as a he-goat with one horn. The first Macedonian king used the unicorn as his standard and flag ensign. So how did the royal coat of arms of Scotland end up with the unicorn rampant as one of its symbols?

"I am going to leave a copy of my book with you today so you can read more at your leisure. But it's not just I but numerous other researchers who are finding one anomaly (to put it politely) after another with the placement of the biblical sites. The conclusion is that none of the countries listed in the Bible, not even one, correspond in any respect to what the authors of the Bible purport them to be. Such is the power of dogma. Constantine created it and solidified it in such a way that no one dared challenge it in over 1,600 years. He even sent his own mother to Jerusalem to salt the pauper's graves there with fake relics to include the cross that Jesus was to have been crucified on. This cross was none the worse for wear after 300 years (it hadn't been cut up for firewood), and now pieces of it are held in veneration in monstrance's across

Christendom. The fakery became the stimulus for the Crusades—one of history's great bloodbaths that went on for hundreds of years—a bottomless pit of warfare and horrors. All the great Christian monuments the Crusaders erected at that time to make the fakery more real. It was Constantine who elevated the desert sandpit called Jerusalem into the center of the ancient and future modern world. He made his capital not Rome, but Constantinople. This was a stepping-stone to the capital Jerusalem, which would be the future global capital of the world. The Flavian emperors and Constantine created the great hoax that created the 'Great Work,' which is the subjugation of all peoples of the world under a one-government, one-religion, one-economy system. The world marches each day ever closer to Constantine's goal, and nothing will be able to stop it because there is the momentum of the ages behind it. The people of the world are never going to be enlightened enough to change this trend. The stories of the druidic nations and peoples would do the emperor's narrative no good up there in the distant British Isles. This was too far away from all the new world power centers and population centers. Those wonderful and compelling stories from the true cradle of civilization they had to confiscate and reapply to a faraway land in order to be of any use. What good are provincial traditions when it's the whole world you are trying to control?

"The Great Work has become an end, and hoax or no hoax, the means justifies the ends, and nothing is to stand in the way. Neither royalty, nor family, nor religion or ideology can stand in the way. In the end, there is only one ideology that counts: that of the Great Work itself—the ultimate globalist Hegelian superstate in which all persons are equal—equal in poverty and prospects and equally enslaved. Only the keepers of the flame of old Rome can ensconce themselves in power to keep all others subservient. And nothing exceptional can they allow. Anything that deviates from the ancient script they will destroy. This includes whole nations, whole races of people. All must die so that the Great Work can live. So what chance does your cult have to change this situation? None."

"Well, I do hope you are wrong about that, young Beaumont. But I do find your line of research fascinating, as I did Powell's. And I must say that it is a great mystery to me how one single man, an image-maker and showman, could sabotage a great new worldwide movement without a plentiful amount of power and resources behind him. His deception has dealt our great religious awakening a very serious blow, I fear. But it is only because his words have been leveraged with power unseen. Your thesis, much to my sorrow, is perhaps the only logical explanation possible. Houdini's conspiracy against spiritualism and its staggering success only seems possible if it draws power from a greater conspiracy, a conspiracy of the ages."

"Believe me, Sir Arthur, it gives me no joy to have to disclose these facts to you. I do not want to tarnish your idealism nor your desire for authentic religion for the people. But I feel it my duty to inform you about what you are up against. Ultimately, the powers that be do not recognize truth or falsehood, evil or good. They only recognize power or the lack of it. It's all about power. They cannot allow anything but their absolute monopoly of it. If it doesn't fit into the script of their hoax upon humanity, that of the Great Work, then they must destroy it, truth be damned, the human race be damned. They care about true religion about as much as they care about the millions who just died in the Great War, or about what became of the Romanovs. Only power is supreme."

Chapter 8

Interview With Dr. Crandon

Sir Arthur was depressed for some time after his visit with Comyns Beaumont. If Beaumont was but half correct with his theories, it was a catastrophe for humanity. For the whole of history to be a hoax for the purposes of a grand conspiracy for the enslavement of humanity is such a cosmic disaster, such tragedy. But the signs and clues are there. "Elementary, my dear Watson," is what Holmes would say. He had been communicating off and on with Dr. Crandon about this topic. Dr. Crandon by now was equally depressed. He had used up all his spare resources, much as Doyle had, for the promotion of the religion that he had so loved. He had exploited his wife also and subjected her to relentless and harsh intrusions into her privacy and personal life. Like they did with all physical mediums, they poked, prodded, weighed, measured, tested, and retested ad infinitum. And even though Margery triumphed over Houdini in the séance room, the public never knew it. They were never told. What the press told them was part of what became the official narrative on the subject—that Houdini was the great protector of the public against these villainous fraudsters who were only out to defraud the public. The unfairness of it all galled Crandon and he, too, turned toward introspection. Doyle and Crandon shared their information.

Somehow they hoped, despite their melancholy, to find their way through this mountain of negativity that fell on them. Somehow he must find a path forward through this terrible cloud in order to see the sunlight again.

The year was 1927. Houdini had died, just as Walter, Margery's control, had predicted. And Sir Arthur Conan Doyle had visited his friend to find a strategy for themselves and the religion that they so loved.

The two men greeted each other without the same joyfulness as before. Now these greetings were more somber and formal. They made their way over to Crandon's study. They sat in silence and looked at each other for an unusually long moment.

Sir Arthur broke the silence. "Well, Dr. Crandon. What do you think?"

"I think that your discussion with Beaumont and previous ones with Powell are right on the mark. There are two types of people in this world, Sir Arthur: those who believe in reality and those who believe in fairy tales. Those who believe in reality believe in the laws of nature and the laws of God. You and I know, we have both seen more than enough, that the spirit world exists just as does the physical but on a different level of vibration, a different diversion. The people who believe in fairy tales believe in an anthropomorphic God, an angry man who lives in the sky on a throne, who judges people and casts down thunderbolts at people who don't believe. History is a struggle between the people who believe in natural law and those who live to believe in hoax. You and I are both depressed because despite all our efforts, it appears that people resent the truth because they feel it confines them.

Therefore, they love the hoax because they feel more comfortable living in a lie. It's bad enough that we live a hoax based on astrotheology. But this hoax Beaumont talks about—this hoax of Constantine's— how are people like you and I supposed to compete with that?

"With the Constantine hoax, you have a master conspiracy that spawns other powerful conspiracies. Without the Constantine hoax, there would be no Catholic or Jewish religions. Those religions have a massive machinery attached to them that have ground their way through the centuries. But once they have served their purpose, the agents of the organization of the Great Work will do away with them. They will create a new one-world religion to take their place.

"Most true believers in the Bible try to see the future of humanity. And they correctly do so. This is because the future is there for us all to read. But it is not because it is divine revelation handed down from that angry old man on the throne. It is because that is what the planners planned for humanity centuries ago. It is the template that the descendants of the original agent for the Great Work must follow. There is nothing inevitable about it all other than that. That is where our hope lies. We don't have to follow this plan, this template, the plan they spell out in the Book of Daniel. In Nebuchadnezzar's dream, Daniel describes the progression of the four empires. The first was the Babylonian. The second was the Persian. The third was the Greek, and the last great empire on Earth was to be the Roman empire. This is where we are now, at the end of that fourth empire. So what's next? Daniel says that it will be the empire that will never end. No one will ever conquer it, but it will destroy all empires of the world and last forever. It is the one-world global government. It is the story of the culmination of the Great Work itself. It is what the Bible has predicted and brought forward to the Great Worker armies of today who are busy bringing it all about. There is no place for deviation from the biblical template. This is another reason why there is no place for exceptionalism.

"All the world must march to the same tune in order to make the Bible a self-fulfilling prophecy. Individualism and personal initiative are the enemy of the Great Work because the Great Work can only function in a collective. And this is the greatest of all the hoaxes. To believe that this false utopia based on lies and myth can ever be more than a worldwide prison for humanity is the height of foolishness. Yet this is what they program people to believe. Spiritual communication, something that those who look for it find a common, not unusual event, is exceptional for the masses. Therefore, it must be destroyed. Freedom and personal liberty are exceptional in history and must be destroyed. Anything that threatens the Great Work the elites must destroy. And the Book of Daniel predicts that they do destroy everything. But you and I know that the book is a hoax. So it is not, therefore, inevitable. You and I are old men. Our time is almost passed. We can hope that the young people coming up, men like Beaumont, can cut through this shroud of lies that leads to our inevitable doom. Because in theory, despite all the machinery, the fulfillment of the Great Work of the old Roman emperors is not inevitable. Whoever expected the Fox sisters to come along and pull back the shroud of spiritual ignorance to give us all a glimpse of the spiritual light? This went contrary to the template. Who is to say that others won't come forward, buttressed by the unseen power of the spirit world, to break the grip of these worldly misguided powers? Didn't the Great Houdini fall to the power of Walter's curse?"

"Yes, I believe he did."

"Well then, the fight is not over yet, my friend. We have all lived under the emperor's curse long enough. Enough is enough. Our time may be up, but my faith in natural law, the law of all the universe, is not shaken. We have powerful friends in spirit. At night when I look out into the sky, I know they are out there helping us. They lived among us, toiled for us, and fought for us. They are not going to see us come to an end which is out of line with the goodness and love of the universe. The substance of the universe is love. Somehow the tyrant's plans must go awry."

"You are right, Dr. Crandon. I, too, believe that this grand hoax of the Great Work and all the lies and hoaxes on which it is based—no matter how old or powerful—is inconsistent with the universe and cannot prevail. The religion of the physical universe is spirit, nothing more. It is not the Earthly avatars or icons. I think you have succeeded in cheering me up, old boy. God bless you."

Chapter 9

Mission Accomplished

In the meantime, back in Rome it was a fine spring day at the Vatican. Monseigneur Roncollo had just finished his breakfast and his morning constitutional through the square and was about to get back to his desk to review the morning reports from overseas. As he reached his office, there stood Father Rossi with a smile and a great look of satisfaction for what he was about to announce to his friend.

"Giuseppe, I got word this morning that you are to meet with your secret contact at the archives today at noon. He will be at the conference area—the same room as your first meeting from several years ago. I hope you can remember which one."

"Oh yes, Father Rossi. I have it in my log written down, but I don't need to look it up. I remember it like it was yesterday."

"Very well then, Giuseppe. Don't get so involved in your work this morning that you lose track of the time."

"That is not possible, Father Rossi. I will count the minutes until the meeting."

"Good luck, Monseigneur. I hope to see you tonight at dinnertime."

And indeed, Monseigneur Roncollo had a new spring in his step, not just today due to news of the meeting but over the last few years that corresponded to the steady improvement in the reports coming from America. His whole aura and demeanor had changed to a most wonderful new look of serenity and self-satisfaction that his friends and associates noticed and appreciated. Gone were the looks of seriousness and furrowed brows. New were the sunny expressions on his face, as if the great barge he was toting all those years had finally reached its destination.

As noon approached the monseigneur wondered who the emissary would be. He hadn't seen Blumberg in over a year, and then only in passing, in an unofficial capacity. He had no official contact with his anti-spiritualist project since his initial contact years ago. Today's meeting, he did not expect. So much time had passed that he expected there to be no further contact. The monseigneur did indeed count the

minutes with great anticipation. Finally, he entered the same conference room in the archives building as before.

At exactly noontime came in his old friend Blumberg. It was he, the same little unpretentious man in his black hat and thick glasses.

"Blumberg, thank the Lord and the Saints it is you! I have seen much less of you these last few years than in the old days when I didn't know who you were."

"That's because in the old days we could just be simple friends. Once our relationship became formal, then everything changed. It is not good for an agent to be seen in an informal arrangement with his client. They always kept a few of us in Rome, just in case something popped up, as in your case."

"Well, in any case, how is your health nowadays?"

"I don't do as much traveling. I am getting old, and traveling is getting too stressful. I will be retiring soon. How are you doing, Giuseppe? You look great!"

"I must say what you and the organization have accomplished over the last several years has added another ten years to my life! The reports from the field just get better and better. What we have accomplished has been a source of great relief and great pride. It is with thankfulness to Heaven and all the Saints that I can declare that our mission is accomplished."

"Yes, my friend, our little mission of getting rid of spiritualism and maybe our big mission too—the fulfillment of the Great Work."

"I can tell you that the brilliant counterattack against spiritualism that Houdini and his intrepid network of agents conducted was breathtaking in its execution and scope. He came within an inch of having the US Congress outlaw the religion altogether. It was just remarkable. Never have I seen one man, a showman of all people, come to wield such power to destroy such a dangerous movement. We tried to exterminate the Muslims with five crusades over three hundred years and failed. But Houdini destroys a dangerous religious movement only armed with the force of his personality."

"And the press, of course," interjected Blumberg, "don't forget the press. We own them and we can make or break anybody through them."

"Well, yes, of course. I don't mean to shortchange any of the assets of the organization that supported Houdini. I just mean to acknowledge that the whole thing was a fantastic achievement."

"Okay, Giuseppe. That's fine. I am glad that we could add ten more years to your life. Before we continue, I must deal with the formalities that you have heard before. First, this meeting has never taken place, and secondly, whatever information I pass along to you is of the highest secrecy, not for you to repeat to anyone outside of the pope himself—and try not to involve him. Have you briefed the new pope on this project yet?"

"No, since the problem was under the jurisdiction of His Holiness Benedict XV, I am under no obligation to brief the new Holy Father. Since the problem no longer exists, I don't feel the need to bother His Holiness with it as he is very busy with current business."

"Very good, Giuseppe, then my obligatory after-action briefing that I am giving you now should be our last and final meeting on the subject. It is the organization's conclusion that we have considerably reduced the threat posed by this cult to you. Our lead agent was, of course, Harry Houdini, who executed the plan with great efficiency. He successfully demonized the cult in the eyes of the public to the point where it should never recover. This low public favorability we can maintain through careful suggestions by the press using the narratives that Houdini forged. Also, it will help on your end to encourage continued denunciations of the cult and coordinate those with other faiths. The threat is manageable now with a small but steady effort for the foreseeable future. A footnote on this subject is the death by natural cause of the woman organizer that you so feared, Cora Richmond. It is our hope that her death will shed many followers from the National Spiritualist Association. It is not certain whether they have charismatic leadership on the same level as she was to replace her."

"Praise be to God! That woman did cause me many sleepless nights, Blumberg. Now I can sleep in perfect peace. And with her passing, I would suspect that people may stop reading her writings. We will work to round them up and burn them. We have faithful groups that will do that."

"Did you have any further questions that you wanted to ask concerning the project? If so, then this will be your last opportunity to ask."

"One thing that bothered me, Blumberg, was the odd loss of Houdini. How does a fit man at the peak of his manhood die, of all things, of a case of appendicitis? That's so rare, especially now with modern medical techniques, that it is hardly fatal nowadays. And the appendicitis was allegedly caused by blows to the stomach? That's totally unheard of! Were these spiritualists who struck Houdini responsible for his death?"

"This is the greatest secret I have to share with you today,

Giuseppe. Under pain of death are you ever to share this with anyone, not even the pope! The truth is that our agents arranged for Houdini's death."

"What? But why?" exclaimed the monseigneur in an alarmed tone.

"Giuseppe, I'm sorry. I'm sure you loved and admired the man as we did. And in your world where you preach compassion, this is a hard thing to accept. But in our world of espionage, where the future course of the whole world is at stake, the value of the life of a single man is nil."

"But why did he have to die, Blumberg? I don't understand!" The monseigneur's voice had suddenly changed from surprise and shock to grief and depression. His facial expression had also changed noticeably from his normal hue to a shade of red with beads of sweat forming above his brow.

"This was a complex case on many levels. I don't think Houdini appreciated the dangers that he was exposing himself to. Unfortunate for his survival, he was a fearless man, so it wouldn't have mattered to him. He may have been an invincible escape artist in the natural world, but he ventured from that into a world that he did not understand or even believe in. The organization analyzed his every move and its impact on the public. And he executed the operation flawlessly until he took on Mina (Margery) Crandon. That's where he failed the mission."

"How so?"

"Mina Crandon bested him. He failed to debunk her. Instead she debunked him. She demonstrated that he was not an impartial observer, but a man with a deep agenda, trying every trick he as a world-famous magician knew to sabotage and character-assassinate her. It became an enormous damage control situation for us. We called in our markers in the American press to cover the mess up and suppress what took place. It was a potential public relations disaster that we had to turn around. This is what ultimately cost Houdini his life. We were unable to save him. Because this round of séances was so high profile with the *Scientific American* committee and the whole world watching, what we needed was a clean-cut debunking of Crandon, like he had done to so many other lesser figures. It is what we needed, but instead we got the opposite. Houdini's hubris is what killed him. He thought Crandon was an easy mark just like all the rest. But she was a whole level above all the rest."

"But why was it necessary to kill him?"

"It was because we knew that he had failed, and what was worse, the spiritualists also knew that he had failed. His failure meant that it might take us another one hundred years to stamp out the cult for good. Houdini's demise was a necessary part of the damage control plan. We needed a martyr to the cause of anti-spiritualism. The spiritualists had their martyrs, and now we needed one in which we could erect a bronze statue to and impress the crowds of people who would come to pay homage at the sacred spot of his tomb. We needed to elevate Houdini to the level of a Christ figure so his memory the masses would always revere."

"How did it happen?"

"Normally, I would not discuss our methods to you because the more you know, the more dangerous it is for you. Old friendships aside, we are engaged in the most lethal of businesses, you and me. One slip of the tongue means a haircut at the neck. It is a very high-stakes game. I hope you understand that. Houdini understood that. He was a veteran agent of long standing. But he always scoffed at the danger to the point where he became one of the very best agents in the history of the organization. But to answer your question directly, we induced his appendicitis surreptitiously by tampering first with his food. The homeopathic serum that his doctor gave him just before he died, unknowingly of course, was the final *coup de gras*. The target date for his death was no accident either. We wanted it to happen on Halloween or the night of All Souls. This would permanently add a sacred holiday to go along with the bronze statue in deifying Houdini for the coming generations and remind all that he was the greatest of all anti-spiritualists. Moreover, we were able to exploit the Canadian pugilists who pummeled Houdini's appendix and imply that they may have had spiritualist connections, thereby indicating that it was the spiritualists who were guilty of his death. Even you yourself thought that. When you are dealing with mass psychology, all you must do is make something sound plausible and the swine will believe it. It's not too difficult. Have you not found this to be the case? We have exploited this defect in human nature, and it has allowed us to exist for hundreds of years. We count on this defect to bring about the Great Work."

"But when you say Crandon bested Houdini, you mean she was for real?"

"Whatever for real is, she was it. You know yourself, Giuseppe, the church has its mystics which they keep cloistered away in convents and monasteries, never to talk to the public. The problem with the spiritualists is that they send theirs out into the public where there is no control. But just look at your children of Fatima. They performed manifestations in front of a crowd of seventy thousand people before the Catholic church got serious and put a lid on it. We can't have anything get in the way of the Great Work—not mediums, not mystics, not little children! So the Crandon woman had control of a real spirit, Walter, who sabotaged Houdini during that disastrous group of séances. You know it happens, Giuseppe, contact with the spirit world has been going on as long as men and women have been walking on this Earth. It is a problem which we have had to keep a constant eye on because it takes away from the narrative that we have constructed for them. Joan of Arc was a great medium, Francis of Assisi the same. It is up to us to manage and act as filter to these individuals to guarantee that none of their revelations ever interfere with our plans for humanity.

"A last consideration was Houdini himself. He had displayed the propensity to be able to betray his benefactors and friends at will. He did this with Robert-Houdin. He did it with Arthur Conan Doyle. He was also addicted to the adulation of the public. Deep down below that invincible ego of his, he knew he had failed with the Crandon séances. And he was a person eager to maintain that high level of public adulation. We felt he might crack at some point if he got to be forgotten in the public eye. He was ruthless when it came to his own self-promotion, and we could not take the chance that he would ever turn on us. As much power as we have with the press, the supreme power is to be able to sell newspapers. Houdini was a master at press manipulation. We could not take the risk of raising a figure so high that we could not bring him down. Remember the first rule of the Great Work—absolutely no exceptionalism allowed! Houdini had risen to a height which went beyond even his own expectations with his anti-spiritualist crusade. He was ripe to demonstrate his mortality which we mercifully helped him to do."

"Blumberg, I am very glad I am not in your business. What you have said to me has already spoiled my breakfast. Maybe it was wrong for me to ask for so many details. I will say a special mass for Houdini and his family. Even though he was a Jew, I know that God will forgive him for all of his faults and accept him into Heaven for helping to save the Holy Mother Church."

"*Oy vey*, you Catholics are just a constant amusement to me. It is that stubborn condescension of yours. It's your version of *chutzpah*. I guess we all need it to be who we are. Someday some being out there will explain it all to us. Is there anything further?"

"No, I am quite satisfied. I will maintain my surveillance over the situation, but from my field reports it appears that the Houdini operation has dealt a devastating blow to the spiritualist movement from which they will not soon recover. They are no longer a threat. The results have been fantastic. It has become a source of great personal pride for me and my life's most important achievement to have been the spark that set the whole structure of heresy aflame. Who in the history of the Holy Mother Church has been so lucky?

And I have you, the organization, and the Great Houdini to thank. God rest his soul! I feel we can conclude now with the two words: Mission accomplished!"

"Yes, Giuseppe, I most wholeheartedly agree. This cult may sputter on for a while, but Houdini did such a hatchet job on it in the press and in the public sphere, the bad taste in the mouths of the people will last for years. And long after you and I are both gone, the organization will make sure that they never rise again. We have always looked upon spiritual contact with the dead as an unacceptable threat. Anything not under the strict control of the government and genuine church authorities is dangerous. Anything that is dangerous to the fulfillment of the Great Work we are obliged to liquidate. I must congratulate you, Giuseppe, for alerting us to this threat which we might have not recognized in a timely fashion. We also owe our gratitude to the late pope. I, too, wish to end with the declaration: Mission accomplished!"

With that final mutual declaration complete, the two said their goodbyes which included a very genuine embrace.

Epilogue

The enemy of my enemy is my friend. Such is the convoluted system that brings enemies of former times—Jews and Catholics—into heartwarming embrace. They have learned to coexist under the greater scheme of things. But as to a religion that has never made an overt threat against either—spiritualism—they can offer neither houseroom nor embrace, but instead seek to exterminate it as one would exterminate cockroaches. Houdini's attacks against spiritualism were uncompromisingly vicious and unrelenting. And this he did to a religion that never did him any harm, and as a matter of fact, had been extremely hospitable to him. In a similar fashion, the attitude of the Catholic church could not have been more hostile to the religion, that again, never meant it any harm. This is a fact, not fiction.

Where we have ventured with this work of fiction is to add other facts such as Crandon's assertion that it was the Catholic church that enlisted the help of Houdini. Houdini the international spy set out not to investigate but to take down the religion of spiritualism forever in the eyes of the public. The narrative that spiritualists are all scammers who are out to fleece the public is one that he created. This narrative he applied to the true believers, like the Crandons, who never had the thought or the need for money. He put the true believers—who had given their lives for the religion that they loved with the same intensity as any other believer in any other religion—in the same category as the fake mediums who he was once one himself. This was a very great evil and injustice. Other religions have their mystics and prophets. Only spiritualism had the machinery that backed-up Houdini singled out for oblivion. To Houdini, his concept of genuine religion was that which was part of that machinery that had been friendly to him. And they felt that communication with the dead was too dangerous to give out to the public in a retail fashion.

It was the Constitution of the United States and its right to religious freedom that spawned modern spiritualism. Only in the United States under a natural law government could such a religion form and thrive. But as this country and the freedom that spread from its shores goes on the wane so, too, will the religion of spiritualism find itself under assault from the globalist and socialist powers. The Houdini conspiracy is very much a part of the latter phenomena.

THE END

Appendix A

Selected Teachings of Cora Richmond from Her Book Psychosophy

(from the Fourth Edition)

Souls

Pg. 109 "Soul is an eternal, immortal, infinite entity, uncreate, in essence like unto God, therefore all souls in the universe have had and will have being forever."

Pg. 31 "At the creation of the universe, souls descend from the celestial world to become live beings in the physical world to animate the physical substance. They thus come from innocence or a potential state and progress to the fully unfolded state to become Angels."

Pg. 31 "Innocence differs from purity in this that innocence is without knowledge, purity is victory, the state of innocence is the state of being tempted, and the matter of material things, in which the soul seeks expression must contain the elements of temptation ... All that is meant by the Adamic fall is that the consciousness of the celestial state, is overshadowed or eclipsed by the consciousness of time or the sense of this Limitation, so that the outward state is not aware of the soul and its inward state."

Angels

Pg. 85 "In the Angelic condition there is no turbulence nor turmoil."

Pg. 85 "No spirits are Angels but when the soul has been expressed in all possible states of mortal life, the recognition then takes place and the Angel is there."

Pg. 85 The dual life (celestial and terrestrial) merged into one become the Angel.

Pg. 86 When the Angel is completed in expression when such as these pass from mortal forms, they are not in spiritual states, but as one Angel enters the Angelic State, which is beyond the spiritual state, the perfection of all spiritual states; they will no more be embodied in mortal form, but will have charge of the souls that come after them, these angels are Parental Souls or Guides.

Archangels

Pg. 202 The Archangel is the Announcer, the awakener who ushers in the tidings of a New Dispensation of celestial light about to take place on the earth, they bid all the Angelic beings to make way and prepare the way for the new outpouring of light. The message comes from the higher heavens to the Angelic Beings that guide the earth as a prophecy. Earthly prophets both true and false arise to declare the coming Dispensation, when the current messianic cycle starts to come to a close, the angels of the closing Dispensation begin to recede from their contact with earth and the Angels of the New Dispensation get ready to come in.

Pg. 203 The Arch Angels are not embodied.

Embodied Angels

Pg. 124 These are Angels that become embodied to do important work on earth, they bear no distinctive mark, mortal's may not even know them in their own household, but they know by the higher Angel's in the Celestial World. It is my belief that Mother Theresa of Calcutta was an example of an embodied Angel. They often end up doing the most important work in society.

Messiahs

Pg.225 The Messiahs initiate each of the 12 Dispensations. There are greater Messiah's and each Messianic cycle has 12 Lesser cycles with Lesser Messiahs.

Pg. 236 Messiahs are archangels who become embodied from the dust of the earth and dwell upon the earth, they are beings of infinite love, wisdom, and power. They come to minister to the human race and transmit the primal culmination of the knowledge of the Dispensation. They usually come at a time of great perversity and intellectual monstrosity or periods of time that lack the perfection that humans are capable of and have given themselves over to every type of deformity and degradation, physical and intellectual. These are periods of the shadows or dark ages in human time. But when the planet is ready, the Great Messiah and the Lesser Messiahs appear bearing the Light of the Dispensation.

Dispensations

Page 227
12 in number, these are given Waves of Light (Perfect Knowledge) by Infinite Intelligence that are revealed truths regarding the relationship of Celestial and Material realms. These waves of light are revelations and not the results of experimentations or deductive knowledge. They come as culminations in the Messianic cycles. They are pure inspiration from within. This knowledge is stamped on the human race by subsequent interpreters.

Knowledge

Page 237
Primal Knowledge is a gift from Infinite Intelligence, not the result of experimentation or deduction. Once this knowledge is given by the Messiahs during a Dispensation it is a permanent imprint. This knowledge may be and is forgotten during the times of shadows which are the dark times in between the Dispensations. However, during times of reminiscence, that knowledge can come back into use. Once the Messianic stamp of knowledge is placed on the human race, it is always possible to regain it.

Progress of the Dispensations

Page 249
Each dispensation takes up the thread of the preceding one and carries it forward with that which the then Dispensation means. Eventually, all the universal information is revealed, the souls ripen and are harvested. Each soul ripens into Angels, embodied Angels and Ultimately Archangels and Messiahs. The point of the ripening of souls' in this process is to provide more workers and creators of

more souls in more galaxies, planets and solar systems in the ever-expanding Universe.

The ripening of the souls through the Dispensations is the catalyst for the populating of the Infiniverse with the glory of Infinite Intelligence.

Times of the Shadows

Pg. 303 Midway between two Dispensations are the times of the Shadows. The tide of knowledge from every Dispensation at some point recedes to leave the earth more encompassed in darkness. The outpouring of great light from the Dispensation uses the darkness in the times of the shadows as the background for the light.

Pg. 304 When the receding tides begin, then the shadows encroach, then the light is growing dim, truth becomes obscured. The institutions of government and religion try to hoard the knowledge gained by the last dispensation and crystallize their power. This is where dogma's and creeds come in. And those who have not been gathered into the Kingdom of Light become intent on putting out the light. It is interesting to note that it is only during the times of the shadows that there is any talk of demons or devils or physical embodiments of evil. During this time darkness rushes toward darkness, error towards error, strife toward strife. The great powers of the world make haste to destroy themselves and each other. It is the terror of the darkness that pervades the world when the tide of the dispensation recedes … Nations, governments, Kingdoms, laws, creeds, are crushed together in conflict and crumble like dust.

In times of the shadow demons and powers of darkness rule the earth and it is not given to angels, ministering spirits or the powers of good to check any portion of this mighty destruction til it shall have had its way, til it has wrought its lesson of destroying the destroyers. Page 310

Where We Are Today

Pg. 313 The Archangel Gabriel closed the Last Dispensation which was the 5th. We have been in the time of shadows since the end of the Mosaic dispensation which was at the death of Christ. As soon as the receding waves of the Last Dispensation begin to pass, the Angels of the New Dispensation appear at their places in the heavens and clothe themselves with the adornments of life to carefully conceal and yet to reveal the Divine mystery that is to come. Seers and prophets are made aware of this while the people of the world bend down to the very depths, seeking in vain for light.

Pg. 223 When the sixth Dispensation begins all past knowledge is to be revealed. The past five dispensations are to be made known. We would put Cora Richmond in the category of a prophet and seer. It is she who has revealed to us that the sixth dispensation is imminent.

Pg. 99 She does not mean today or tomorrow, but the signs and tokens she says are in our midst. She says; "the light that has been foretold is coming as it dawned over Egypt, as it dawned over Assyria, as it dawned over Jerusalem, such is the light that is now coming over you." This dispensation must be nameless until the Messiah appears. Because the Sixth Dispensation finishes one half at the cycles of religion upon the earth, one half the messiahs, so this dispensation is to be more important and complete. Page 100

Appendix B

Spiritualist Talk Explaining Cora Richmond's Teachings

What does it mean to be authentically human? What does it mean to lead an authentic human existence? Most people never ask themselves this critical question. Why? Because they are too busy leading lives that are programmed by others. People get too busy trying to satisfy their basic needs. They are controlled by their bosses and authorities of all kinds. They don't have the time to consider why they are here living in the physical world. The reality is that we are all part of an intricate divine plan whether we want to believe it or not. We can either accept our part now and save ourselves a lot of trouble later, or we can go on in denial that we have a part to play in the divine plan.

Our founder, Cora Richmond, the first vice president of the National Spiritualist Association of Churches, revealed the divine plan to us in her writings with inspiration from her guides, back in 1888. She wrote a book called *The Soul and Its Embodiments*. The soul is the primary spiritual building block in the universe. We are all the product of our soul, and the soul is never satisfied until perfection is achieved in every direction. Life as an expression of God—Infinite Intelligence—was not intended to illustrate imperfection, but to seek and attain perfect expression. And the work of the universe of life is understood when divine love and wisdom are attained. And without the promise of the perfect victory in all directions, human life would be a dismal failure.

We've all witnessed the perfect victory, and we've all relished in it and admired it—whether it's the baseball pitcher who pitches the perfect baseball game; the gymnast who achieves the perfect ten score at the Olympics; or the perfect symphonies by Mozart, Bach, or Beethoven that appear to be timeless examples of perfection in music. We all admire examples of perfection like this. It gives us chills when we see them. It takes our breath away when we witness them. This is what it means to be authentically human. It is the hope and the promise that we, too, can achieve perfection. There are two challenges in the attainment of our own perfection. The first is inspiration. The second is interfacing the inspiration that comes from Infinite Intelligence and combining it with the physical world to achieve the perfection that we all aspire to deep down in our beings. The process of developing our own gifts is what it means to be authentically human and to achieve an authentic existence. We are out to be all that we can be as a part of human nature, but we are tempered through the mill of natural law. The process is ongoing and inevitable.

Cora Richmond talks about the Angels of Light that dispense this light, this inspiration from Infinite Intelligence that we use to create our world. There are twelve spiritual ages which the Earth must go through to reach a point of spiritual perfection. These are the twelve dispensations. At the beginning of each dispensation, the Angels of Light infuse us with all of the spiritual knowledge that we need to achieve this perfection and authentic human existence. The problem that arises in these dispensations is that we are not evolved enough to maintain or hold that light all at once. That's why there are twelve infusions of light, or dispensations of the divine light. We see evidence of this amazing burst of light and knowledge in archaeology. The Great Pyramids of Egypt, for example, were constructed with forms of high technology that we are still unfamiliar with thousands of years later. The architecture of Machu Picchu was constructed by a method of welding stone together to such a perfect extent that scientists today are unable to explain it or duplicate it. There are many such pieces of evidence that you have to refer to the alternate historians, alternate archaeologists, and other alternate experts who have found concerning the ancient societies like Atlantis and Lemuria and other societies that were built due to the light of the initial dispensations.

But between the dispensations are the times of the shadows. This is when people through their institutions, governments, and religions try to keep the light from slipping away. These institutions become crystallized by dogmas and creeds. The governments and churches become tyrannical, and the world sinks into a new dark age of tyranny and death. The initial triumph of the dispensation turns to tragedy, and the world awaits its new period of messianic rebirth.

But after each period of dispensation the survivors have an increased ability to hold more light than they were prepared to do after the last period. We are currently caught between the fifth period and the sixth. The last dispensation ended after the period of the Vedas, the wisdom of Confucius, the periods of Moses, the Buddha, and Jesus. Today we have weathered the storm of two thousand odd years of the time of shadows, when darkness came over our world. We are awaiting and living in the time of the New Dispensation, when the old dogmas and creeds fall away, and the new period of light brings us to a new world and a clearer connection to spirit. This time we will experience a new spring, a new period when gifts of the spirit, signs, and wonders will become commonplace again. Allopathic medicine will become one with spiritual healing. A more perfect form of communication with the spirit world will come about and mediumship will become the primary source of our knowledge. The floodgates of life and light will open, and the dawning of the New Age will bring us to a new time of openness and freedom devoid of selfish pursuits. Humanity will advance on a whole new level of morality when swords will be beaten into plowshares, and people will rejoice in the perfection of the universe and the principles of natural law and the love of Infinite Intelligence which will be embraced by all.

But we don't have to wait for the complete enfoldment of the New Dispensation from spirit to take effect—we have all the tools necessary to bring humanity out of the darkness now. The advent of modern spiritualism is a sign of the New Dispensation to come. Furthermore, it is the birthright of every human being, every divine spark of the Creator, to live an authentic human existence which includes the manifestation of the gifts of the spirit.

This time is here now. Look for its signs. Know that the dark period that we witness in our world today is quickly coming to an end. The dogmas and creeds are fading away. The period of secrecy and conspiracy of the tyrants is coming to an end. Their time has ended. The trumpets of the Angels of Light are about to sound— they are sounding now every time people discover their connection to spirit and discover their authentic humanity. A new dawn is upon us. The light is beginning to burst over the horizon. Embrace the light and know that your freedom is at hand. Thank you and God bless.

Appendix C

A Spiritualist Talk On Houdini

The job of the historian is to search for causes as to why things happened the way they did. Then they argue about it with other historians and occasionally come up with a consensus view that is generally accepted by all as to why something happened. So I'm going to put on my historian's hat right now and ask the question: whatever happened to spiritualism? When I look at the spiritualist camps, like Camp Etna, I see that a mere hundred years ago these camps were packed with thousands of people. Camp Etna had over three hundred cottages and a capacity of over ten thousand people's attendance for a summer's day event. Today these camps are little more than recovering ghost towns in comparison and are making a slow and gradual comeback. One must ask him or herself what happened, and why? Why the great collapse? Were its people losing faith in religion overnight, or was it the result of a planned assault from outside forces? I would like to explore this question for today.

The high-water mark of modern spiritualism in this country was just after the Civil War. This was a time when more than ten million people, or roughly 26 percent of the population, professed to be spiritualists. That's so very hard to believe now. The Judeo-Christian establishment at the time was enormously threatened by the potential loss of their hegemony over the population by what they perceived to be an upstart homegrown cult. That they had tried everything to squash the threat is well documented. But people weren't listening to all their woofing and hellfire from the pulpit. It wasn't until the 1920s that they finally found a champion they could rally around. He was a Hungarian Jew born in Budapest, Austria, a rabbi's son by the name of Erik Weisz, who had immigrated to the US in 1878. After reading the autobiography in 1890 of the French magician Jean Eugene Robert-Houdin, Erik Weisz changed his name to Harry Houdini. In 1908 he wrote a book of his own on Robert Houdin in which he denounced his mentor as a liar and a fraud. But to briefly summarize the career of Houdini, he became famous as a handcuff magician and a stuntman. He was also a stunt aviator and appeared in silent movies. He did whatever it took to promote himself. He became highly connected in the United States Government and in governments overseas. A book was written on him a few years ago that exposed his ties to the US Secret Service, a precursor to the modern-day Central Intelligence Agency. Houdini was in fact an international spy who reported back intelligence from his world travels. But this wasn't his crowning achievement.

Houdini's crowning achievement in his career was to take down the religion of spiritualism which he did almost single-handedly. His crusade to debunk spiritualism was also his greatest contribution to establishment religion. His spy work required him to befriend the famous people in foreign governments in order to extract information. Likewise, he set out to befriend famous spiritualists like Arthur Conan Doyle. Conan Doyle had abandoned his detective story writing which had made him world-famous in order to pursue his research into spiritualism in which he became a devout follower. Houdini used his friendship with Conan Doyle for publicity and to get connected with all the elite spiritualists. Then, all of a sudden, as Houdini had done before having turned on his idol, Robert Houdin, denouncing him as a liar and a fraud, so he did the same to his friend

Conan Doyle and his wife. Thus commenced Houdini's final quest for superstardom.

Houdini went on a grand tour with a team of hired investigators and agents to track down and humiliate spiritualist mediums across the country. Some mediums he caught in the act of producing fake materializations using magician's tricks. But contrary to popular belief he did not prove all to be fake. His efforts to debunk Margery Crandon were inconclusive even though they were reported otherwise in the press. Houdini was able to rationalize everything in his own mind as to what he saw. But as all good mediums know, spirit cannot be commanded by the skeptics. This is what skeptics choose to never understand. Houdini could not command spirit to perform miracles any more than King Herod could command Jesus to turn water into wine. Houdini used all his talent and showmanship to try and drive the stake through the heart of spiritualism. Established religion was the beneficiary and could finally give a sigh of relief over the negative advertising exploits of Houdini against the religion of spiritualism. And these exploits were on a scale that would make Madison Avenue advertisers proud.

The skepticism of Houdini knew no bounds. He was a skeptic's skeptic. Ultimately, he concluded that there was no connection between the living and the dead. There was none possible. Furthermore, there was no evidence that the spirit world even existed, unless he could see it on his terms and presented to him on demand. Houdini went to his grave saying that if it could be possible, then only he, the Great Houdini, could make it possible. He gave his wife Bess certain codes and formulas to be used for communication after his death. A few brave mediums came forward to try and crack those codes, but none were successful.

To begin to unwind all the damage that Houdini did not only to spiritualism but to religion in general, you have to go back to establishment religion. This is because if mediumship were impossible in its various forms, then the miracles of Jesus would have been impossible also. Mohammed's night journey from Jerusalem up to the seventh Heaven would also have been impossible. Even Erik Weisz's own tradition of Judaism would have not been possible because Moses could not have parted the Red Sea, nor produced manna from Heaven. So, in other words, using Houdini's infallible skepticism, establishment religion would be debunked and would have been impossible. Why? Because if Harry Houdini couldn't do it, then it couldn't happen. But Houdini never had anything to say about established religion and their claims of materializations, and he never attacked any other religion besides spiritualism. And established religion was overjoyed that they had in Harry Houdini a stalwart champion because they knew that the public would never make that leap between Houdini's skepticism and the supposed miracles that were the basis of their traditions. Margery Crandon once said that the Vatican had enlisted the help of Houdini in the anti-spiritualist crusade.

What is Houdini's legacy? What does he represent? Houdini's doctrine of absolute skepticism does not uplift humanity one iota but instead condemns it to the shadows of ignorance forever. By debunking all mediumship, he disempowers the whole human race for all time from any type of true spiritual knowledge. By denying the power of spirit in everyday life, he has stolen all hope of anything beyond the purely material existence with no hope of a life hereafter. When they put your body in its grave, that's it—nothing follows. With that negative belief, life itself becomes a prison, an ultimately meaningless exercise, to quote Shakespeare: "a poor player full of sound and fury signifying nothing." In such a world, only the establishment religions ensconced in centuries of hegemony over their subject populations—with their temples, mosques, and churches standing like mighty fortresses demanding blind faith and obedience to their dogmas and decrees—have a right to exist. There is no room individuals taking responsibility for their own spirituality via communication with the spirit world;

they are a threat to the existing order. This is the legacy of the Great Houdini.

The reason for the initial exuberance for modern spiritualism was because it was a new paradigm that resonated with all independent thinkers and people who listen to the voices deep within themselves. Modern spiritualism resonated because it was based not on man's law but on natural law. It was based not on blind obedience to an anthropomorphic godhead but to spirit itself. Just the words "Infinite Intelligence" turn the concept of the anthropomorphic godhead around. God is not a man riding a white horse, or an all-powerful angry white-haired man sitting on a throne judging and condemning people to eternal hellfire for the mistakes and misdeeds of their life. This is the creation of the established religions and their mind control programs over the centuries. Infinite Intelligence is the light of the universe, far too big to be contained in one anthropomorphic being.

Houdini's legacy makes one group of people happy—those who don't want to take responsibility for their own spirituality while they are alive and who are too afraid to contemplate where they will be going when they are to die. Houdini's universe encompasses only the visible spectrum of light which is less than 1 percent, while spiritualism concerns itself with that and all the rest.

The problem with skepticism and skeptics is that they reject evidence that does not fit their preconceived notions of what is real. These preconceived notions are the result of their upbringing and their psychological development. Some people, for example, will not question the religion they grew up in. If they find evidence to the contrary about the validity of this religion, they automatically reject it. Just about every religion calls themselves the "true religion." But they can't all be. Their followers keep claiming absolute truth because to do otherwise would be to insult their parents or grandparents. The skeptic will always reject evidence that conflicts with his or her beliefs. Harry Houdini's mind was not open to anything beyond the physical realm.

So, to answer the question of whatever happened to spiritualism, the answer is that it never survived Harry Houdini's onslaught. His mass advertising skills and showmanship, along with the blessing and support of established religion, successfully derailed the modern spiritualist movement. Only today is a second wave of interest in spiritualism back on track and making a comeback from the plague of skepticism that Houdini's assault released. The comeback has started due to the failure of mainstream religion. Not even Houdini's showmanship has been able to drag them over the finish line. People today are spiritually unsatisfied and are reaching out for something new, something that empowers them and is not a distant hierarchy of spiritual elites. They want a concept of God that they feel safe in believing in. Truth has a way of coming out. It cannot be suppressed forever. And religions based on the whims and fantasies of the spiritual elites are based on a foundation of sand while those based on natural law are built on a foundation of stone. God bless.

Appendix D

Spiritualist Philosophy

Where is our true home? Home is a place where you feel comfortable. It is where you eat, sleep, and maintain yourself. When we go to a friend's house and they want us to relax, they may tell us to feel at home. When we think of home we think of a physical place such as an apartment or a house. Whatever one's feeling of where home is, there is one truth that we always overlook: our true home is nowhere on this physical world or in this physical universe. Our true home is in the spirit world.

We have a funny way of looking at things. We look at everything the opposite of the way we should look at it. When we think of a person, we think only of their physical body first, then we think of their personality. We hardly ever think of a person's soul or spirit. This is because we cannot see it. We live in a world that the five senses rule. And the ego rules over the five senses. Because fear rules over the ego we tend to think that only what the five senses tell us is real. But this is not true. The five senses tell us that the physical world is what is real. This is also not true. When you see a person, you are not seeing that person in their true form. Their true self is their etheric body which animates them but which you cannot see. A person's physical body is but a temporary home to a person's spiritual body which lives forever.

Materialism is the great opponent of spiritualism. We live in a world that the materialists dominate because the ego is what drives us in this direction. The ego lives in constant fear because physical life is temporary and all of us are destined for physical death. Fear causes the ego to spend all its resources focused on the physical world that it detects through the five senses. This is why we, as spiritualists, have a difficult time making others see the value of our religion. The physical world to the materialist is everything. There is no need for them to come to grips with the spiritual aspect of life until life's circumstances force them to when physical life comes to an end. But in the meantime, ego drives them to many excesses. Greed, anger, and jealousy are all products of an ego that considers only the physical world as real. The materialist is a predator in this world. Only the person whose spirit rules has any concept of morality and ethics. This is because the person who lets his spirit rule over the ego knows that life on this Earth is not real life because it is not permanent. The only things that are permanent are the spirit and the soul. When our bodies pass into the spirit world, the only thing we can take there with us is our character which we have forged from this temporary home. The kind of person we have become is what we take with us. This includes the times when we have been kind, loving people. If we have not shown love or kindness we take that also to our permanent home, our real home, the home where we will abide forever.

Perhaps therefore we are born into this false world of the physical. It is a testing ground and a learning ground for what is to come when we get to our real home. We will carry whatever light we have produced here. If we have been selfish and self-centered, we will carry that light with us. If we have been giving and self-sacrificing, we will carry that light with us as well when our souls find appropriate spheres which will be our real home.

So, people wonder, why are we here? Why is the physical world even necessary? People of the Zen religion recognize the voidness of all life. They recognize the illusory nature of the physical world. All of us must someday give up our physical bodies to go back to our real home, the spirit world. And it is not just people who must do so—*all* societies, all civilizations must one day give up their substance and come to a time when even the memory of their once greatness, their very existence, will one day be forgotten in time. Moreover, the planets will one day cease to be. Our sun will one day cease to exist along with its solar system. Whole galaxies will come and go in time. And the truth is that only the spirit world is infinite and permanent. So, some of us wonder, what is the purpose of it all?

And as serious spiritualists know, the answer is in one simple statement: as above, so below. The point of physical existence is to bring it in harmony with the natural love of the spirit world. In the spirit world, there is *no conflict* and *no ego*. Out of death comes new life, and it is the message of spirit that the love that exists there must be brought here. It is the message of the spirits in that world to make the physical world full of love. It's that simple. Near-death experiencers who have had a glimpse of that world know this. The tragedy of the physical world is the tragedy that fear and ego bring to this world.

Our founder of the NSAC, Cora Richmond, talked about the successive waves of loving light and knowledge that are to come to this world. These waves of light from the spirit world bring us closer to what we were meant to be. The point of progress in this physical world is to bring us to a deeper understanding of all things. We were brought to this world to achieve moral perfection, not just physical or intellectual perfection. Morality is the humble act of embracing natural law. Natural law encompasses all law. With acknowledgment and living in accordance with natural law, we achieve the highest levels of perfection. With moral perfection, we achieve happiness for all time. Our mission and purpose as human beings is to achieve happiness through harmony with nature's physical and spiritual laws.

To achieve this happiness, we must learn the importance of spirit and its ultimate triumph over ego and fear.

It is no accident that the teachings of our church have taken place in this country, the United States. This country allowed its people the freedom to develop mediumship in an open and public platform. This is because it was founded by a group of freethinkers who believed in natural God-given rights. It had no state religion and allowed the free flow of religious information, unlike other nations that believed in enforcing rigid dogmas and doctrines. The NSAC that Cora Richmond founded has a structure and a government but is based on its subservience only to God and natural law.

Societies come and go, nations come and go, but only universal natural law is supreme and infinite. Our bodies die and have their end, but our spirit lives on to ultimate perfection. The mission and point to life here on Earth is to come to the realization that only spirit, not ego, is permanent. We have our lessons to learn, we have our mistakes to make, but the goal for all of us is the same: universal love of all things above and below.

The challenges of life are great, but so are the rewards. The knowledge that we achieve in this life becomes a crown of light that will always be with us. I had a situation lately when looking into the military records of my uncle who fought in Europe in the army during World War II. I know through my parents that he had seen much action fighting in Europe. Unfortunately, I found out from the National Archives that his war record was destroyed by a fire in 1973. So no one will ever know the extent of his service for our country. The only one who knows is my uncle and his comrades who are now in the spirit world. His struggles and sacrifices changed his young life and formed his character. Although his records are gone, the experiences he went through will forever be with him. I only know of the kindly gentleman whom I saw. I will not know of the horrors he no doubt experienced of death and war. He came here to fulfill that mission at that time for the growth of his spirit and soul. And with the passing of his life, his goal he had achieved.

So his life came full circle. After the drama of life in this physical world, he is now home in his real home. So it is with all of us. We are alive today to face all the challenges that life brings. Those challenges shape our character that will be the only thing we get to take with us when we pass. So our purpose is clear. Our mission is to become more moral beings finding the path to happiness and contentment each day by living our lives in accordance with nature's physical and spiritual laws. And rest assured that we will achieve that goal one day when the time comes to go back to our true home in spirit. God bless.